Desperate, Mo[...]
to excuse her [...]
Servius Antonu[...]

"Of course you must go," he said brusquely, setting his scroll on the marble tabletop. "Servius Antonus is an important man. He has numerous connections in the senate. And those on the senate have the ear of Nero."

Stunned, Moriah looked at him, scarcely believing her ears. "What of Mother? Surely you cannot expect me to attend a banquet when she is in such ill health."

"Lydia shall not improve," he said, and the light seemed to go out of his eyes with the words. His mouth narrowed. "You are nearing three-and-twenty years of age, Moriah. It is well past time I made you a match."

"Servius Antonus?" Moriah relived his bold stare raking her at the games and felt she might be sick.

"Not necessarily. But it would not hurt for you to be seen. The guests at Antonus's feast are certain to be some of the most important people in Rome. . . ."

Moriah kept silent as he continued to explain the advantages of her attending such a banquet. For her to argue further would hinder her cause. She had been raised to be subservient and to accept the decisions made for her, whether she approved of them or not. How she wished that Paulus were here! He could talk to his uncle and urge him to change his mind. Usually Clophelius listened to Paulus.

Sudden memory of his failure to sway Clophelius concerning her attendance at the games caused Moriah to close her eyes in dismay. It was then that she knew her fate was certain.

PAMELA GRIFFIN lives in Texas and divides her time among family, church activities, and writing. She fully gave her life to the Lord in 1988 after a rebellious young adulthood and owes the fact that she's still alive today to an all-loving and forgiving God and to a mother who earnestly prayed that her wayward daughter would come "home." Pamela's main goal in writing Christian romance is to encourage others with entertaining stories that also heal the wounded spirit. Please visit Pamela's website at: http://members.cowtown.net/PamelaGriffin/

Books by Pamela Griffin

HEARTSONG PRESENTS
HP372—'Til We Meet Again
HP420—In the Secret Place
HP446—Angels to Watch Over Me
HP469—Beacon of Truth

The Flame Within

Pamela Griffin

Heartsong Presents

Thank you to my faithful friends and critique partners—both past and present—for your encouragement and willingness to help me on this project. To my precious sons, Brandon Christopher and Joshua Aaron, I pray that no evil will ensnare you, that you shall endure to the end, and that you'll always know, without any doubt, that God is real.

As always, I dedicate this book to my loving Deliverer, my Rock and my Fortress, my God, *El Elyon,* who hides me under the shadow of His wings, so that no destruction shall befall me.

A note from the author:
I love to hear from my readers! You may correspond with me by writing:

> **Pamela Griffin**
> **Author Relations**
> **PO Box 719**
> **Uhrichsville, OH 44683**

ISBN 1-58660-682-4

THE FLAME WITHIN

The Flame
Within

Dear reader:

To keep true to the time period of the story, included is some material that may be considered objectionable for young readers. Although biblical Rome was much worse than is depicted in the following pages, I tried to tone down scenes as much as possible without detracting from the plot or emotion of the story. However, parental screening is advisable before giving this book to young readers.

My prayer is that this book will encourage you to hold fast to your faith in Jesus Christ, no matter what fiery trials you may come up against.

Thank you and God bless,
Pamela Griffin

prologue

41 A.D.

The slight figure escaped through Rome's meandering streets, a wrapped bundle clutched against her wool tunic. Hearing the steady approach of hobnailed sandals, she darted into a side street and pressed her back against the cool marble of a temple.

Sweat beaded her forehead while she waited for the soldiers to pass. Tears spilled onto her cheeks, and her chest heaved with the tortured breaths she barely contained. After agonizing minutes, the sounds of marching trailed into the distance. Night insects again took up their incessant chirps.

She darted away from the wall, her bare feet stinging as they slapped the jagged flagstones. At another narrow road, she turned a corner and rushed up a short flight of stone stairs, through an archway, and across the main street known as *Via Appia* to yet another side street. The house of Dinoculus could not be much farther. Surely she would find it before anyone could stop her!

Nighttime was her ally, its thick darkness enfolding her in a shielding cloak. Yet the sliver of moon etched against the sky reminded her of something sharp and ominous—not unlike the shape of a weapon the gladiators used in the arena during the games.

She shivered and drew the bundle closer. Her weary legs moved with more speed, though her muscles throbbed and her feet bled. In her haste, she had left her sandals behind.

At last she reached a set of stone stairs cut into the ground. They led up a steep incline to an imposing building—a symbolic structure revealing the wealth and stature of the family who resided there. She hurried up the hill but tripped on a step.

7

Alarmed, she flung out her hand to break her fall, twisting her body around to protect the bundle. She lay still for a moment, breathing hard, heart racing. Ignoring the stabbing pain in her side, she forced herself to rise and resume her climb.

At the top, a burly servant appeared out of nowhere and barred her way to the entrance of the house. Dancing light from a torch anchored high on the rock wall cast his face into eerie shadow. "Why have you come? What business have you at this late hour?" He reached for his curved scythe hanging from a wrapped belt at his waist and gripped the handle in a most threatening manner.

"Oh, please," she gasped, wresting the hood of a man's cloak from her head. "I must speak to your mistress! Have mercy!"

A scowl covered his features. From beneath his jeweled turban, he looked at her with black bottomless eyes. His frightening gaze dropped to the wrapped bundle clutched to her chest, and his bushy brows drew down farther.

The girl swallowed, seeing she was about to be denied entrance. "I beg you, if you will only tell your mistress that Helena has sent me. . . ."

He stood silent as though considering. "Wait," he commanded before turning away.

She exhaled a shaky breath of relief at his curt order. She was not being refused. If she had been, she had no idea where she would have gone. Certainly not back to the *insulae* belonging to former tribune Rexus Caspus. It was no longer safe at the tenement.

An eternity seemed to pass while she waited, fearful, her gaze repeatedly going to the dark street with every noise she heard. If her petition were denied. . .surely death would be her reward.

one

Twenty-three years later

Lost in thought, Moriah strode along the corridor that surrounded the *peristylium,* allowing her fingers to brush the marble columns along its open sides. She approached the center of the roofless courtyard and sank to one of the stone benches. A two-tiered fountain bearing the sea god Neptune riding seven golden dolphins stood nearby.

Leaning closer to it, Moriah trailed her fingers through the cool water and glanced at the lotus blossoms floating atop the surface. Beyond the open arched door at the rear of the house, a more elaborate garden had been added at her mother's request, and Moriah lifted her gaze to its entrance. There, thick shrubs, stately trees, and myriad flowers saturated the sun-drenched outdoors with color and greenery. Here in the courtyard, plants also grew in abundance, complementing the frescos of outdoor scenes along the walls. From the branches of a fig tree, a dove cooed.

Moriah sighed. Why was she not happy? She was the daughter of one of the wealthiest men in Rome, and though her father held no place on the senate as Flavia's father did, he was a well-respected author of highly acclaimed books. Even the emperor was said to enjoy her father's writings.

Noticing that the ends of her dark hair now brushed the ground, Moriah straightened. She flicked back her one, rope-like braid of thin braids intertwined with the pearls Sahara had woven into the strands, so that it again hung down her back and to her hips. It confused her that Flavia Valerius Decima, a family friend whom she'd known since childhood, seemed so much happier all the time.

9

Brow wrinkled in reflection, Moriah watched a red-and-blue butterfly, its wings as beautiful as rare jewels, land on a nearby grapevine. Perhaps "happy" was not the word she sought—though Flavia most assuredly possessed an insatiable desire to enjoy life to its fullest.

"Tell me, Butterfly," Moriah lamented. "Why can I not be more like Flavia? Why am I so dissatisfied with life and what it has to offer?"

The lovely winged being flitted away through the garden door as though it did not care to listen to her self-pity another moment. Moriah could hardly blame the creature.

With an impatient sigh, she traced the circular pattern of the mosaic tiles with the toe of one sandal. Perhaps she should go to the games at the amphitheater with Flavia one time—merely to see what all the excitement was about. Her friend constantly tried to persuade her to attend them. Flavia always seemed to be talking about this gladiator or that one, always in love with the hero of the day, the one with the most kills to his credit.

Moriah shivered though the flower-scented breeze flowing throughout the courtyard was warm. The games had long been the way of Rome's entertainment, and the chariot races at Circus Maximus were no better. It seemed the people never tired of watching endless parades of criminals, gladiators, and charioteers spill their blood for Rome's pleasure in gruesome feats of which Flavia had excitedly informed her friend.

Moriah closed her eyes at the memory. No. She would not go to the games. She could not fathom how watching someone die could be pleasurable, though she would never divulge such an admission to Flavia. The woman already thought Moriah too naive, and Moriah supposed she was right.

Moriah seldom left her father's house. When she did, it was to journey to the market with her maid or to the forum with Flavia. As a child, she also had visited the villa in the country with her parents, though such outings were now rare. Mother had been ill for years and required her daughter to stay close by, despite the fact that she did have personal servants to attend her. Surprisingly, Father allowed it, though Moriah was two years past the age limit for being wed. Most Romans were fined if they were not married by the age of twenty, but Moriah knew that her father had used his influence with Senator Valerius so that any fee was waived.

Moriah further pondered her existence. She supposed she did prefer her life, even if it was dull compared to Flavia's reckless mode of living. At least it was safe within these high walls, and she did not have to concern herself that Father might accept, on her behalf, any unwanted offers of marriage to the crude men she'd met at the forum. Such as the man Flavia had introduced her to last week.

At the memory, Moriah again shivered.

As if thoughts of her friend conjured her up, Flavia breezed through the curtain hanging over the arched portal and into the courtyard. "Greetings, Moriah."

"Flavia!" Moriah rose from the bench. Flustered, feeling as if the woman had actually known what was running through her mind, she spoke. "Why are you here?"

"Do I need an excuse to visit?" The blond pouted. "Moreover, is that any way to greet a friend?"

"No—no, of course not," Moriah said. Flavia always did have the ability to make Moriah feel infantile with a few words or a look. "My apologies."

"Never mind. I have fantastic news. Your father has given permission for you to attend the games!"

"The games?" Moriah repeated, horrified. She slowly sank back onto the marble bench. Was it coincidence she'd been thinking about Rome's entertainment only moments ago? Or a terrible omen? "No. . ." Her response came out in a whisper.

"Yes—is it not exciting?" Flavia took a place beside her, seeming oblivious to Moriah's distress. "Now that your mother is faring well, your father told me it is time to introduce you to the world of Rome." She gave a bright laugh, clearly enjoying Moriah's stunned reaction.

Moriah blinked, uncertain how to respond. She saw no way to escape the situation, since her father had declared it and she was duty bound to abide by his wishes. Yet there must be some means to refuse the invitation without risking his ire.

"Would you care for refreshment?" she offered weakly when she became aware of Flavia's fixed gaze.

The blond gave a disinterested toss of her head. "I prefer stronger wine than what you have. Besides, I cannot stay. I am traveling to the *ludus* for a private showing. . . . Would you care to come with me, Moriah?" she added sweetly, a wicked gleam lighting her eye. "I am certain it can be arranged."

"No. Perhaps another time," Moriah added when her friend's thin brow arched. The words sounded weak, a ploy to change the subject, and Flavia likely knew it. Moriah had no desire to accompany her to the training camp of the gladiators—now or at any time in the future. The school was open to visits from fans and citizens who had money and power, as Flavia did. With her, nothing proved impossible.

At twenty-five, Flavia was twice divorced and once widowed. She had long worshiped at the temple of Venus, goddess of physical love and beauty, and was involved in numerous liaisons—some with the gladiators, who were given a pregame feast on the night before their death matches. Flavia often insisted that Moriah accompany her, but Moriah offered her excuses each time, as she did for all the other questionable events to which Flavia invited her.

"Hmmm. Well, if you are certain." Flavia gave a careless shrug. Catching sight of the handsome slave Aidan coming toward them with a platter in his hands, she rose from the bench and cast a knowing look at Moriah. "Then, too, if I had such a slave attending my needs, I would rarely leave my father's estate."

Annoyed, Moriah watched Flavia study Aidan's muscular arms and legs—displayed to perfection by the short white tunic he wore—then lift her gaze to his broad shoulders and deep chest. A tooled leather-and-studded-brass belt adorned his trim waist, and a silver slave bracelet encircled his upper arm.

Knowing Flavia as well as she did, Moriah could almost hear the thoughts revolving inside her head: *How had one such as he escaped being sold as a gladiator? He has the face of Apollo and the body of Mars. What I wouldn't give to spend an afternoon with him. . . .*

At Flavia's close scrutiny, Moriah felt herself redden, as Aidan was presently doing. Flavia let out an incredulous laugh.

"A man who blushes—what an amusing rarity. I may have to buy him from you, Moriah. He piques my interest." She ran her pale ringed hand lightly over the front of his tunic.

"He's not for sale!" Moriah blurted. Seeing Flavia's look of shocked surprise at her uncharacteristic outburst, she added, "What I meant to say is, he's not mine. He is Father's slave, as are most of the slaves in this household. You would have to consult him, and I doubt Father would part with Aidan. He has served him well for many years."

"Hmmm. A pity," Flavia murmured thoughtfully, lowering her hand to her side and looking intently into his eyes, which stared at the fountain beyond her. She turned with a shrug. "I must be going. Five days and the games begin. I will send my litter for you one hour after sunup."

Moriah gave a distracted nod, and Flavia disappeared through the curtain. Something about the expression that had been in her eyes troubled Moriah. What was Flavia planning? Would she use the fact that their fathers were best friends to her advantage and try to purchase Aidan by asking her father to intervene? Knowing Flavia as well as she did, Moriah realized her purposes in securing him would be for her own pleasures.

At the thought, a hot shaft of pain burned through her heart. Moriah looked up at Aidan. He stood, holding a platter with a silver goblet and narrow-necked pitcher.

"My lady." His deep voice warmed Moriah and sent shivers down her spine at the same time. "Deborah asked that I see to your refreshment and thought you would care for something to drink."

"Yes, please." Moriah studied him while he set the platter on the bench and poured honeyed water into the goblet. Her mouth was dry but not from thirst. Her mind clouded as it often did from his nearness, and she did not even think to ask why Deborah was not attending her.

Flavia's earlier interest in Aidan caused Moriah to look anew at his features—appearing as though they'd been sculpted from marble. His deep blue eyes seemed to hold hidden secrets, and his hair of burnished gold was not cropped short like that of the men of Rome but rather grew to his shoulders. He had the body of an athlete—lithe, muscular, strong—and curiosity overcame her usual shyness for a moment.

"Aidan, how came you to be in my father's household?"

He looked surprised by the question. After handing her the goblet, he stared past her, focusing on a nearby fluted white column twined with ivy. "The servant in charge of the slaves purchased me nine years ago from the slave auction, intending to use my services for the master in equestrian forms. When the master had the accident and could no longer sit a horse. . ." He paused, as if sensing Moriah's discomfort over her father's crippled state. "I was made into a house servant."

Moriah took a sip from her goblet while studying him. She wished the rule her father had issued for his household—stating a slave could not look into his master's or mistress's eyes—had been banned. She did not consider it a form of disrespect as he so obviously did. How she longed for Aidan to look at her! To truly look at her.

Embarrassed by her thoughts, she lowered her gaze. "You may go."

"My lady." He bowed in deference.

Moriah watched him walk away, his stride like that of a lion. Regal, assured, with an air of quiet grace. Who was Aidan? He was different from any slave Moriah knew. Strange. He had been in this household a long time, and only in recent years had she begun to take notice of him. Was it because she was now a young woman and looked at everything with eyes of love?

Irritated with the endless stream of unanswered questions her mind had formed this day, Moriah set her goblet down with a bang and stood to her feet. Restless, she moved through the garden door and began to stroll along one of the paths, allowing the sun to warm her shoulders.

Once girlhood left and her body took on a womanly form, Moriah had begun to receive offers from the men she met at the forum. Yet they were frequently crude and deserved no serious consideration. Neither did Moriah engage in tawdry affairs, so common among the people of Rome. It was odd. She was born a citizen yet despised the wickedness of the city, though she'd seen little of its practices. Still, Moriah knew the lewd acts that Flavia had described could in no wise be called love. But surely not everyone in the city was corrupt, frequently traveling from one relationship to another as the butterfly did from flower to flower. There must be someone out there who felt as Moriah did and sought only one person with whom to share his life.

Yet to this day, no man of Rome had caused Moriah's heart to pound erratically from his nearness, while at the same time giving her a feeling of comfort in his presence. No man, that is, except for a slave from Britain.

Was she mad?

Moriah exhaled a weary breath and stopped to pluck a rose from a nearby trellis. Twirling the velvety petals against her cheek, she returned to the *peristylium* deep in thought.

❧

From the dark recesses of a nearby portal, Aidan stood hidden behind a gathered curtain and watched Moriah, his heart full. The linen material of her ankle-length white *stola* was draped in elegant folds about her slender form, giving Moriah an added air of grace.

She had unusual-colored eyes for a Roman; they sparkled as clear and blue as the Mediterranean Sea and held a tinge of violet. Her hair reminded Aidan of the coat of a panther, black and shiny, and her complexion was as fair and smooth as ivory from Ethiopia. Often he witnessed envy in women's eyes when they looked upon Moriah. Yet her true beauty lay in her innocence, her purity, her sweetness—qualities so seldom seen in Rome. The woman Flavia was also physically lovely, in a harsh way, but could not begin to compare to Moriah. At least not in his estimation.

Aidan grimaced, his hand flexing against the drape. He strongly suspected that Flavia's insistence concerning Moriah's attendance at the games could lead to no good. After the head servant Hermes had accompanied Moriah and Flavia to the forum last week, he'd told Aidan that Servius Antonus— a powerful man in Rome and also one of Flavia's former lovers—had approached, displaying a strong interest in Moriah. It was said the middle-aged man had an appetite for beautiful virgins.

Aidan clutched a fistful of the crimson curtain. Yet what could he do? He was a slave, powerless in his role. He could not say or do a thing. . . . No, that was not entirely true. He did have one effective weapon, a weapon he had learned the value of many times.

Aidan stealthily moved to a small, secluded arbor at the back of the garden against the wall. Kneeling on the ground, he lowered his head to his hands clasped on the stone bench. Often he prayed for Moriah, but never before had he felt the need so strongly, as he did today.

"Heavenly Father, I ask You to shield my lady and protect her from the evils of this wicked empire," he whispered. "Help her to stay pure in the midst of such moral decay. I ask that You open her eyes to Your truth, Lord, and open her heart to receive Your Word—"

A snap cracked the air nearby. Aidan stopped midsentence and hurriedly stood, realizing the danger if someone discovered him praying. Though Roman law did not prohibit Christianity, tensions flared in opposition to it, and each day that passed, the hatred increased. Many considered his faith a form of treason against the empire. In this household, especially, his master thought ill of Christians, and Aidan continually had to guard his tongue.

He exited the arbor, taking careful note of his surroundings. Everything appeared normal. Likely it had been a squirrel scampering through the bushes or perhaps Moriah's cat. Yet what if it had not been something so harmless—and bore not four feet, but two? Troubled, Aidan went to seek out his master before Clophelius sent someone to find him.

28

Moriah moved along the colonnaded walkway to the two shallow steps leading into her *cubiculum,* her sandals clicking on the mosaic tiles. Barely offering a glance around the simple luxury of the quarters that comprised her bedchamber, she moved across the room and pulled aside the crimson drape with an impatient tug. She took the three wide steps to the enclosed terrace—another addition her mother had insisted on for each bedroom, much like their country estate in Capua, with its many balconies.

Placing one knee on the couch beneath the window, Moriah leaned her forehead against the lattice screen and put up a hand to touch the diagonal strips of wood that covered the opening.

Rome. Her city. So why did she feel as though she didn't belong? Had never belonged. Even more peculiar was the sense that she didn't feel a part of this household, either.

Moriah exhaled loudly in irritation and lowered her hand, weaving her fingers through the lattices at waist level. Certainly her tumult of emotions left much to be desired this day! Brooding, she threw open the screen and scanned what she could see of the busy streets far below.

Numerous Corinthian columns and arches decorated the many limestone buildings scattered throughout the Seven Hills of Rome. The carved marble blazed ivory in the noonday sun, which burned against a cloudless sky of pale blue. Bold colored marble ornamented some of the temples with red, yellow, and black, and terra cotta eaves adorned many rooftops.

In the valley, Moriah could see part of the *Forum Romanum* in the distance, where people strolled to exchange news and gossip. Opposite the capitol, at the end of the road called *Via Sacra,* the marketplace bustled with activity as storekeepers hawked their wares. Scrolls of books, precious metals, jewelry, silks, wines, leathers, fruits, and more—everything anyone could possibly desire—was found there. Columns of a temple high on the opposite hill gleamed golden in the sunlight, as though promising wealth and good fortune to all who visited. Moriah watched as a group of people, appearing like tiny insects, climbed wide stone stairs to make offerings to their god.

"My lady?"

Moriah started at the soft voice. She turned and offered a faint smile to the petite woman who was more sister than servant, though they were not related by blood. Noticing the sleepy look in the sepia-brown eyes, Moriah shook her head. "Deborah," she chided, "you are weary. You must rest."

The Jewess studied Moriah closely. "Perhaps you are the one in need of rest, my lady. You look as though you are under great strain."

Miserable, Moriah glanced at the people crowding the streets. "Flavia told me she secured Father's permission for my attendance to the games. But I do not wish to go! However, if Father says I must, I have no choice in the matter." Again, she whisked her gaze to Deborah's. "Is that not so?"

At the hopeful plea in Moriah's voice, the servant put her dusky arm around Moriah's shoulders. "Perhaps if I rub scented oil into your temples and sing for you, it would help, my lady?"

"Yes. Please do. If I can think more clearly, I might be able to establish some method to approach Father and not have him refuse me."

Deborah retrieved an *alabastron* of perfumed oil. She sat on the rose velvet cushion of the narrow couch, instructing Moriah to lay her head in her lap.

Moriah did so. At once, Deborah's firm yet gentle fingers pressed into her temples, massaging, comforting. The spicy-sweet perfume from Arabia permeated the air, making Moriah wonderfully drowsy.

Softly Deborah began to sing one of many songs she often did—songs that stemmed from her faith. This one, Moriah noted, was about a young boy named David who fought a giant named Goliath and saved his people from tyranny.

As Moriah slipped closer into blissful nothingness while listening to Deborah's melodic voice, her mind envisioned the scene, and the face and form of the courageous David took on the image of a male slave from Britain.

two

Clutching the sides of her *stola*, Moriah hurried along the corridor and down the few steps to another corridor. Her nap had caused her to be late for the evening meal, something that was sure to displease Father. What terrible timing! She would need Father in an agreeable—or at least approachable—mood before she asked him to reconsider her attendance at the games.

Swiftly moving into the *triclinium*, Moriah saw that her parents reclined around the low circular table. Ignoring her father's frown, she hurried to one of the empty bronze-ornamented couches that could easily hold three people and also reclined upon her side. Here, as in all the rooms of the house, boldly colored blocks of marble in geometric patterns and numerous frescos of gods and goddesses, satyrs, and cherubs decorated the walls. Sensing her father's continued disapproval, Moriah focused on the colorful wall painting directly across from her—this one of a sacrificial calf being brought before Apollo and Artemis, who watched with approval.

A servant approached with sweet figs. Moriah selected one from the platter while another slave filled her goblet with watered wine. Moriah flicked her lashes briefly in her father's direction. Solemnly he stared at her, and her mother seemed in no better spirits. Heaviness settled over the atmosphere, not relieved by the sweet sound of the lute and panpipes played by two Greek slaves in the corner of the room. It was a relief when the guard and doorkeeper, Jacabar, came at the beginning of the second course to announce the arrival of Centurion Paulus Seneca.

"Paulus!" Moriah abandoned the cushions of her couch, unable to contain her excitement. Her handsome cousin strode into the room, his red cape billowing behind him. Like

20

a little child, she ran to him and threw her arms about his leather armor before he'd walked halfway into the room.

"Oh, Paulus! It has been so long," she chided, "and not even a word! Did you forget us?"

He laughed, pulling her arms from around his neck, and gently set her from him. "I plead innocent, little dove. We have only just returned."

"Moriah," her father reprimanded. "Come away and let Paulus catch his breath." He looked at his nephew. "Stay, eat with us. You must tell me the latest news. I hear so little of it these days—only what Senator Valerius tells me when he visits." He motioned for a slave to bring another goblet and plate.

Paulus strode to the couch where his lame uncle reclined, with his aunt next to him. "Greetings, Uncle Clophelius, Aunt Lydia." He clasped his uncle's thin arms in a fond gesture, then bent to deliver a kiss upon Lydia's pale cheek. "I would be honored to eat *cena* with you after I divest myself of my armor."

Fondly, Moriah watched Paulus move toward a small anteroom. The months had been good to him. Lines around his mouth had deepened, but he looked as hearty as ever, and his wavy hair still showed no signs of gray. Looking back on her childhood, Moriah was certain she'd been an awful pest to Paulus, since she had idolized her older cousin. Yet he treated her as a doting brother might have. Now Paulus was a centurion in the Praetorian Guard, assigned to protect the emperor, and had little time to visit. Still, Moriah was proud of him and his accomplishments in the most elite branch of the military.

Once a slave removed Paulus's cape and the rest of his armor, leaving him clad in his short tunic and sandals, Paulus returned to the table and reclined next to Moriah. He took a long look at her and smiled.

"You are as lovely as ever, Cousin," he murmured for her ears alone. "Venus herself must look with envy upon one so beauteous as you, and surely she turns her head away in shame."

Moriah's face warmed. "You mock me, Paulus."

"Never. I speak only words of truth." Paulus's gaze softened and rested on her a little longer than usual.

Perplexed, Moriah shook her head. "What is it, Paulus?"

"What?" He seemed addled. "It is nothing." Quickly he took a long drink from his goblet and set it down. He then proceeded to tell the family what he knew of the latest news concerning their emperor.

According to Paulus, Caesar had spent much time in Antium, writing prose and resting his voice upon the urgings of his senators. On several occasions, he gave performances in the cities—Naples and others—to the people's delight. That Nero presented himself as a ridiculous buffoon rather than the highly gifted artisan he supposed himself to be was a fact all who valued their lives kept to themselves.

Still, Moriah pitied their emperor. He had recently lost his only heir, an infant daughter, to a sudden illness. From Flavia, whose father was often summoned to Nero's court, Moriah had learned how ecstatic Nero had been at his daughter's birth and how devastated he'd been by her death. His wife Poppaea, a former harlot despised by the citizens of Rome, was convinced the babe died from an enchantment placed on her head.

Moriah puzzled over this as she picked the tender flesh off her honeyed squab. She had long ago lost faith in the power of the gods and goddesses. Had not Mother visited the household idols in the *lararium* and given wafer offerings each morning, praying for favor and protection for her household? She gave offerings at the temples, as well, for the healing of Father's paralysis and for her own health, especially to Aesculapius, god of healing. And still Father was lame and Mother was often ill.

No matter what the people did, it appeared as though the deities rarely showed favor, being difficult to please—if in fact they existed. Moriah was uncertain what to believe anymore and wondered if Poppaea's theory of enchantment was well founded or if there were supernatural powers at work in people's lives at all.

"You're not listening, Cousin."

Startled out of her musings, Moriah looked over at Paulus and blinked. "What?"

He laughed and held his goblet out for a slave to refill with the weak, honeyed wine. "I asked what you have been doing of late."

She hesitated only a moment. Here was her chance.

"Flavia petitioned Father that I be allowed to attend the games. And Father has agreed." Her gaze flicked down to her barely touched food, making it obvious to all present that she shared no such desire.

Paulus looked across the table at his uncle. "Perhaps Moriah is not yet ready—"

"Nonsense!" the older man boomed. "As a daughter of Rome, she has a duty to fulfill."

"A duty?" Paulus asked, confusion evident in his tone. "Since when is it a duty to attend the games?"

"We will talk no more of this," Moriah's father commanded. "I have made my decision."

Paulus's mouth narrowed. He turned to Moriah, the expression in his eyes going gentle. "Would you feel more at ease if I arrange it so that I can go with you?"

"I would appreciate that—yes." Hope flickered but was just as quickly doused. "It is not possible. Flavia told me that she will be sending her litter for me. The arrangements are made."

He waved his hand in careless dismissal. "I will send a messenger to inform her of the change of plans. We can take my chariot."

"But Paulus, what of the ban?" Wheeled conveyances were not allowed on the city streets during daylight hours. Had Paulus forgotten in the months he'd been away?

"The ban does not include a soldier's chariot, Moriah," he said with an indulgent smile. "It applies to lumbering wagons and carts of merchants."

"Oh." Slightly embarrassed at her ignorance concerning such matters, she grinned. The prospect of her beloved cousin's company appealed to Moriah much more than an afternoon with the surly Flavia. Still, it would not be wise to annoy her friend. Because Flavia's father was close to Nero, he wielded power—and Flavia wielded power over her father. He gave her anything she asked of him.

That realization made Moriah think of Flavia's interest in Aidan, and she hastily spoke. "Nevertheless, I do not wish to cause offense—though I would much rather go with you. Perhaps we should at least sit with her." Sudden memory of the conflict between Flavia and her cousin hit Moriah, and she rued her thoughtlessness. "That is—if you are agreeable?"

Paulus gave a distracted nod, his gaze going to the platter of grapes in front of him. "I am agreeable." Yet his expression had become dour.

No more was said, and Moriah looked away. She wished now she had never spoken.

ॐ

Late in the night, Moriah rose from her bed, unable to sleep. She slipped a silken robe over her short *tunica* and padded to the entrance of her room. Pulling aside the drape, she glanced at the quiet *peristylium,* then moved down the colonnaded walkway to the garden door. When slumber evaded her, the peaceful arbor, bathed with the delightful scent of exotic flowers, lulled her into rest.

Before she could reach the garden, raised voices inside the *bibliotheca* alerted her to an argument. Moriah recognized her father's commanding voice and her cousin's equally authoritative tone. Curious, she moved to the entrance of the library and put her ear to the curtain. Becoming conscious of the fact that she was acting childish by eavesdropping on a private conversation, Moriah turned to go, but the mention of her name stopped her. Now more than a little interested, she stepped close and again put her ear to the drape.

"You have no right to speak to me thus concerning Moriah,"

her father shouted. "Her affairs are not your concern!"

"What possible difference could it make whether she attends the games or not?" Paulus questioned just as angrily. "You know how she sorrows to see anything harmed—a bird, an animal, especially a person! Why would you force her to do this thing?"

"I have my reasons, and I repeat, Paulus, they do not concern you. So leave it be."

"Nay, Uncle, I cannot do so. I love Moriah and only want her happiness. Can you say the same?"

Tears pricked Moriah's eyes at the silence that followed. It was no secret to her or to anyone else in the household that her father never had held her dear, though he'd always provided well for her. She could not fault him that.

"Paulus, there has been much talk. Every month another edict is issued for some poor soul to cut open his veins or fall upon his sword under Caesar's orders."

"Senator Valerius has shared this with you?"

"Yes, and more as well. It seems word of Moriah's beauty has reached those on the consul, including an important patrician by the name of Servius Antonus. Need I say more?"

"Antonus," Paulus spat. "What I would do to him if I were able. May Pluto take him to rot in the underworld! I've heard much concerning his reputation."

"His reputation is no worse than that of countless other citizens in Rome."

"Which says much for our fair city," Paulus responded cynically. "But enough of the snake Antonus—what has he to do with Moriah?"

"Servius has asked questions of Valerius concerning her. You will remember that he and Valerius are related, though not by blood. And Servius knows the senator and I are friends."

"And Valerius's daughter is Moriah's friend, as well—and a former lover of Antonus, who is likely the one behind this sudden interest for Moriah to go to the circus. By all that is sacred, Uncle! You cannot seriously consider allowing as rare a gem as

Moriah to mingle with such company. Allowing her to be in the presence of Flavia, I understand, though only marginally. I know her father is your friend. But *Servius Antonus?"*

"Your defense of Moriah is admirable. But tell me, Paulus, do I detect a note in your voice of a more personal nature?"

Moriah's ears burned. Yet she couldn't leave now if her life depended on it.

"She is my cousin. And as dear as a sister to me," Paulus said more quietly.

"But you know, Paulus, she is neither of those things."

Moriah gasped, then put a hand to her mouth to avoid detection. What did this mean?

"I am an officer of the Praetorian Guard. I cannot marry."

"Yes, it is so. Still, I sense that you do not intend to make guarding our emperor a lifelong career."

Paulus let out a disgusted snort. "Is it not better to fight in Armenia or Judea or even build roads in Britain than to be part of a retinue to a singing puppet?" There was a pause. "No. I've not yet decided. But you have deviated from the issue. We were discussing Moriah, not my career or plans for the future."

"Yes, but tell me truthfully, Paulus. Are they not one and the same?"

Trembling, Moriah moved away from the curtain, confused by all she'd heard, fearful to hear more. She hurried across the courtyard and to the arched door leading to the lavish gardens. Opening it, she slipped through and inhaled a steadying lungful of cool air. Yet, the heady fragrance of roses did not help relieve the conflict of emotions that assaulted her.

Swiftly Moriah moved down the path, the moon guiding her way. She approached her arbor, almost completely hidden by grapevines and secluded from the rest of the garden. Needing the comfort of its solitude, she hurried inside the dim interior—and stumbled over someone's kneeling form.

"Oh!" She put her hand to the ivy-covered wall, trying to maintain her balance.

Aidan hastily clambered to his feet. "My lady! Are you

hurt?" His hand went to her upper arm to steady her.

"I—I didn't see you," she stammered, aware of the heat of his hand searing her arm through the thin material of her silk robe. His hair shone pale in the moonlight, but it was too dark to see the rest of his features clearly. Yet Moriah sensed that those intriguing blue eyes were staring directly at her. The thought unnerved but excited her. As close as he stood, she could feel the warmth radiating from his body. This closeness did strange things to her insides, making her feel as though she might melt while at the same time making her feel vibrantly alive.

Aidan released her arm. "My apologies," he said gruffly. He moved as if to go.

"Why are you here, Aidan?" Moriah blurted out, not wanting him to leave.

He turned, his face still hidden in shadows. What seemed an eternal pause elapsed before he spoke. "I was praying."

"Praying?" Moriah sank to the bench, her shaky legs no longer able to support her. "To which god? I see no statues or idols here."

Aidan paused another long moment as if uncertain he should speak. "To the one true God," he said at last.

"The one true God?" A fearful, almost hopeful, tone laced her words. "Does He have a name?"

"He has many names. Some call him The Most High; others call him the great I Am. He is the First and the Last, the Alpha and the Omega—"

"The beginning and the end," Moriah translated.

"Yes, my lady. Through Him all things were made, in the heavens and on the earth. He created the universe and all that is in it, even the world in which we live." Aidan hesitated. "He sent His Son to show mankind the way to salvation, and it is through His obedience to death on the cross that all men can be saved."

Prickles of apprehension raced up her spine. "And does the Son of this God of yours have a name as well?"

There was another pause, then Aidan said quietly, "His name is Jesus, the Christ."

She inhaled sharply. "You're a Christian!"

"Yes, my lady, I am."

At his soft reply, Moriah felt sudden alarm, though instinctively she knew she had nothing to fear from Aidan. In his presence, Moriah often experienced a strange peace she had found nowhere else in Rome, with the exception of her maid Deborah. Aidan certainly did not look as though he belonged to the bizarre religious sect notorious for eating human flesh, killing babies, and causing all manner of difficulties in Rome. It was said that the Christians were the ones poisoning wells and starting riots. They pledged allegiance to their God, excluding all others, even Caesar. A dangerous thing to be sure.

Moriah deliberated between dismissing Aidan and telling him to stay—a small part of her curious, even somewhat desperate to question and hear his answers.

A slamming door in the distance broke the silence. She rose quickly. "I must go. But I wish to hear more about this God of yours another time." Realizing how many in Rome despised the Christians, her father included, she assured, "Your secret is safe with me, Aidan. Be at peace."

"I am grateful, my lady."

Moving to the entrance of the bower, she awkwardly tried to brush past. He pressed his back to the wall to give her more room, but still their bodies made slight contact.

"Thank you," she said in a breathy whisper without lifting her gaze from the ground. She hastened away, her robe billowing behind her.

☙

"Oh—try again, Sahara. It simply is not right!"

Impatient, Moriah plucked golden pins from her elaborate hairstyle, allowing the dark locks to fall down her back once more. She looked in the polished metal of the hand mirror at her mother's Egyptian maid standing behind her. Tense lines framed the full mouth, and the kohl-blackened eyes snapped with frustration.

Sahara was one of the finest hairdressers in Rome. Moriah's

mother had secured her services not long after she married Clophelius. He bought Sahara from a friend for a high price, claiming he wanted only the best *ornator* for his wife. Yet, today, nothing the Egyptian did seemed to satisfy. Sahara had already dressed Moriah's hair three times, and Moriah was about to explode from frustration. A young Syrian slave came to Moriah's side and held up a *stola* of mint green for her approval. Moriah was not pleased.

"Not that one, Sinista!"

The girl's brow furrowed. "Pardon, Mistress, but you told me to bring it to you only moments ago."

"Well, I changed my mind." Moriah's words came out clipped. "Bring me something in blue. . .no. . .lavender. Flavia may well say that she considers amethyst appropriate only for royalty, but surely lavender is not so bold it would be considered unsuitable for the daughter of Clophelius Dinoculus! Bring me what I ask. Go!"

Sinista and Sahara looked in confusion to Deborah, who sat quietly in a corner, observing Moriah's unusual behavior. At the Jewess's nod, the servants fled the room. Heat rushed to Moriah's cheeks. Discomfited, knowing she had behaved abominably, she averted her eyes and turned on the stool, again lifting her mirror.

Deborah approached. Placing her hands on Moriah's shoulders, she met her gaze in the cloudy reflection. "What is the trouble, my lady? Surely this does not only concern your revulsion at attending the games?"

Tears stung Moriah's eyes. Needing the assurance of her friend, she spun around on the ivory inlaid chair and clasped Deborah hard around the waist. She rested her head on her bosom, as she had done when she was a child.

"Oh, Deborah. I heard Father and Paulus talk the other night, and they said strange things, unusual things—things I cannot begin to understand."

Deborah stiffened. Her hand stopped stroking Moriah's back. "What sort of 'things' do you speak of, my lady?"

Moriah told her and fearfully looked up at her maid. "Do you know why they spoke so? I do not know the man, Servius Antonus, nor do I wish to. I made his acquaintance only once at the forum and found him repulsive. Moreover, why should he care if I attend the games—and even arrange it with Flavia so that I would? And whatever did Father mean when he implied that Paulus is not my cousin? Is he the adopted son of my uncle Marcus?"

A pained expression on her face, Deborah cradled Moriah's cheeks with both hands. "Oh, Child. You are still so young and innocent, though you are a woman well grown. Perhaps your mother and I were wrong to shield you. Perhaps we should have told you—" Abruptly Deborah broke off.

"Told me?" Moriah blinked in confusion. "Told me what?"

The woman sobered and straightened, lowering her hands to her sides. "It is not for me to say, my lady. I have said too much as it is. If you want answers, you must ask your mother or father."

"Mother has recently recuperated from her last bout of illness, as you well know," Moriah argued. "I fear she is not strong enough, nor do I think Father would tell me should I ask." She grabbed Deborah's hand, tightly clasping it between both of hers. "Please, Deborah. Tell me wherein the mystery lies. I must know. Do I not have the right? Especially since it concerns me?"

The look in her eyes uncertain, Deborah drew a deep breath, and Moriah waited, expectant. But her hopes were dashed when her maid slowly exhaled and shook her head. "Forgive me, my lady. For me to speak would be to reveal a confidence. You must ask your mother. She will tell you what it is you wish to know."

Frustrated, Moriah released Deborah's hand and turned away. The two slaves timidly reentered the room and were obviously relieved to discover Moriah had calmed and switched to brooding silence.

Sahara fashioned Moriah's hair in several elaborate intertwining ropes at the back of her head. Catching up the rest of the locks, she then halved them and wove tight bands around the two sections, placing them inches apart at the nape of her neck. One thick section was brought over Moriah's shoulder to fall past her waist, the ends of her hair curling. The other trailed down her back. A narrow headband of intricate gold was placed near the back of her head like a crown, fitting close to the scalp.

"This style pleases me, Sahara," Moriah murmured, though her heart was not in her words. "You have done well."

The Egyptian bowed her head in reply. Deborah lifted a flask of red ocher by one of two twisted handles and pulled the bronze spatula from its mouth, but Moriah put up a hand to stop her. She wanted no adornment of cosmetics. This day she would much rather be outfitted in the rough woolen garb of a poor plebeian, if she had the choice and it meant she could escape her fate, than be dressed in fine silks and forced to attend the games. Let her go looking pale and wan. It did not matter.

Sinista hesitantly moved forward with a filmy *stola* of the palest lavender. Moriah rose and stood as motionless as a marble sculpture, allowing the woman to slip the dress over her short *tunica*. Golden clasps were fastened to the material at each shoulder, leaving the arms bare. A long cord of the same lavender was attached to the clasps to cross between her breasts and tie around her waist.

Deborah brought a *palla,* and Sinista fastened the thin cloak to Moriah's right shoulder with a brooch. The *palla,* a couple shades darker than the *stola,* was then brought under Moriah's right arm and arranged in a beautiful drape. Wrapped loosely around her back and shoulder, it ended in billowy folds that hung over her left arm. Gold and sapphire earrings and necklace finished the ensemble. Because a great deal of walking would be involved, Moriah opted for her soft leather shoes rather than her flimsy sandals.

A young slave girl rushed into the room. "My lady, Centurion Seneca awaits."

Moriah's heart increased a beat. After the conversation between her cousin and her father the other night, how would he treat her?

When she reached the *peristylium,* Paulus smiled, took her hands in his, and kissed her cheeks in a brotherly fashion, relieving her mind. "Shall we go?" he asked.

"I wasn't aware that I had a choice." Her words were bitter, though she tried to say them lightly, and Paulus looked at her with understanding.

Moriah caught sight of Aidan moving along the corridor, carrying a huge amphora on his back. Bent over as he was, he appeared not to notice her. She wished she could call out to him, but what would she say?

As though he discerned her stare, Aidan turned his head without releasing his hold on the clay vessel. For several earth-shaking seconds, he looked fully at her, then turned away. Moriah watched him continue toward her father's rooms.

Paulus studied her, then stared at the retreating slave. His mouth a thin line, her cousin tightened his hold on her elbow and turned her toward the atrium. "Come, Moriah, it is time."

Never had five small words filled her with such dread.

three

Outside, the day was hot. Moriah scowled at the field of cloudless blue above her. If only it had rained, perhaps the games might have been cancelled. But the Fates obviously were not on her side.

Paulus assisted Moriah as she stepped up to the chariot. He took a place behind her, grabbed the reins tossed up by a young slave boy, and gave the order for the white Arabian stallions to proceed. They drove through the streets leading to the valley between the Palatine and Aventine Hills. People on foot quickly parted to make room for them or risk being run down.

A surge of exultation swept through Moriah to feel the breeze on her face, though the air was filled with every odor imaginable, from the sweet smells of fruits and flowers to the stench of fresh manure and unclean bodies. Still, riding in Paulus's chariot gave her a wonderful feeling of freedom, which unfortunately lasted only a short time. All too soon they pulled up in front of the gigantic oval stone building of the Circus Maximus. Flavia waited near one of the entrances.

"There she is," Moriah murmured to Paulus.

Flavia stood underneath a shade a slave held over her, her gaze impatiently roaming over the men in white togas and women in colorful *stolas*. Golden hair was wrapped in elaborate coils around her head, and the *palla* she wore was a medium hue of the lighter green of her *stola,* matching her eyes.

Once Paulus gave his reins over to a slave, he took Moriah's elbow, and they made their way to Flavia. The look of relief that crossed her face was intense.

"Moriah, I thought you would never arrive! Of course, the preliminaries have not yet started, and they are rather dull at times. However, Servius has been most impatient, to the point

I finally told him I would stand outside and wait for you. We are to sit in his private box."

Flavia turned eyes full of longing tinged with bitterness toward Paulus. Moriah knew long ago he had spurned her advances—something one did not do to Flavia Valerius Decima.

"Hello, Paulus," she said, her chin lifted. The tremor in her voice belied her aloofness.

"Flavia."

Paulus's cool stare and the curt way he spoke her name made it clear his feelings had not altered. Flavia's mouth tightened, and she looked down at Paulus's hand cupping Moriah's elbow. Her rapier sharp gaze raked Moriah with green splinters. "Come," she said, her words clipped. "Servius awaits."

Turning on her heel, Flavia strode past clusters of people and through the high arched door. Evidently the man in charge of seating recognized her. He did not try to stop her, nor did he ask to see her chit as she stormed past and tersely said, "They're with me," while motioning behind with a flip of her hand.

Moriah clutched Paulus's arm and followed the haughty blond. Tiers of benches crowded with spectators surrounded the oval arena and were separated by open passageways and sets of steep stairs. In the center stretched a long low wall covered with monuments. Seven bronze dolphins and seven bronze eggs stood at each end.

Paulus noted the direction of Moriah's stare. "They are used to count laps for the chariot races. The gladiatorial games are typically held in the amphitheater at Campus Martius, but since several races are also scheduled for the day's events, they will be held here instead. You may not remember, since you never attended the games, but when I was younger, I took part in the races."

Moriah remembered. She suppressed a shiver, thankful her cousin had not been killed in the dangerous sport. Horrible tales of men falling from their chariots and being dragged by horses at breakneck speed around the arena or the frequent and fatal crashes of chariots was news Moriah often heard.

"The seating is on different levels," Paulus continued and looked at the seats above the passageway directly across from them. "The poorer plebeian sit at the top, while the aristocracy and senate sit above and next to the imperial box, near Caesar." He nodded to a group of men whose togas each bore a broad purple stripe denoting them as senators. "The wealthier you are, the closer you are allowed. Still, many patricians have their own boxes." It was to one of these boxes Flavia led them.

Moriah studied the man who sat on one of four chairs in the small enclosure. A servant held a shade over his head; another filled his goblet with deep red wine. With his curly dark hair and in his white toga, Servius Antonus was somewhat attractive, she supposed, though his face was pale, a bit flaccid, and faint dark rings lay under his eyes. Such flaws could not erase his aristocratic features or commanding presence, however.

As he had done at the forum, Servius stared at Moriah with feral blue eyes—the eyes of a predator. And she felt like the prey. He frightened her, and she wished she were anywhere but in his box. How thankful she was that Paulus was with her!

"Moriah, how good of you to join me." Servius arched a thick brow as he turned his gaze toward Paulus and noted his embroidered tunic set off by an ornate leather belt. "Centurion. Off duty?" His words were casual, though a menacing undertone laced them.

The corners of Paulus's mouth lifted, though the smile did not reach his eyes. "The opportunity to accompany my cousin during her first time to the games was one I could not refuse. There are many undesirables from whom she should be protected."

Servius's eyes narrowed as he correctly interpreted Paulus's barbed statement. He opened his mouth to speak, but at that moment the sharp blare of trumpets sounded throughout the arena. Moriah took the seat farthest away from Servius, with Paulus next to her and Flavia between him and their host. Moriah did not chance a look in Servius's direction but could sense his displeasure in the seating arrangements.

She stared at the arena, feeling a thin stream of excitement mingling with the dread. Flavia had said the death matches would not begin until hours from now, and it was all a matter of pomp and circumstance at the beginning, which suited Moriah well. Pomp and circumstance was highly preferable to bloodletting.

She looked toward one of the gates where a chariot entered, led by four gray horses. A short, fat man standing inside waved to the crowd, while a tall Numidian slave held the reins and stood behind him. The chariot began circling the arena. Other chariots followed, banners flying, carrying gladiators who would perform later. A line of gladiators trailed them on foot, two abreast of each other, as well as other men associated with the games.

Paulus leaned toward Moriah. "The man leading the parade is the sponsor," he spoke near her ear. "If he takes too long with his speech, the crowd may jeer and throw partridge bones or apple cores at him."

Moriah glanced at her cousin and sensed by the look in his eyes that he hoped for such a thing. She hid a smile at this hint of boyish mischief inside the tough soldier.

As she watched, the entire parade circled the arena, finally coming to a stop before the emperor. The sponsor, who was announced earlier as Sigellinus Caldonius, made a flowery but short speech that seemed to please Nero, who inclined his head graciously toward the financier.

Sigellinus then turned toward the gladiators and raised his hand in signal. The combatants, many wearing bronze helmets with yellow or red plumes as well as various pieces of armor and cloaks of purple and gold, strutted in front of the crowd, who called out to their favorites. Men and women alike became hysterical when their gladiator stood before them. They shouted, each calling out a gladiator's name and trying to bring his attention their way. Some of the women suggested obscene things that made Moriah's face burn from embarrassment.

The entire spectacle disgusted Moriah. She closed her eyes, wishing she were back at the house, while the crowd continued to roar. Soon she felt Paulus's hand cover hers, and his voice spoke in her ear. "You can look now."

Opening her eyes, Moriah found the gladiators had moved to stand before the emperor's box. As one, they lifted their right arms stiffly in the air in salute. "Hail, Caesar!" they shouted. "Those who are about to die salute you!" Quickly they turned and reentered the gates to await their turn at battle.

Paulus leaned close to Moriah. "Now comes the amusement."

From all sides, deformed men and dwarves scurried into the arena. They bowed to the emperor, then turned to fight the person in front of them with their soft leather swords. The crowd laughed at their antics. The mirth heightened when a dwarf jumped onto the back of a fallen man with one arm and slapped him repeatedly with his mock weapon. Delight filled the faces of some who pointed and stared at something in the middle of the arena. Moriah turned to look. With his leather sword raised high and flapping as he ran, another dwarf chased a hare down the length of the circus. The sight was somewhat amusing, and Moriah felt a fraction of a smile lift her lips, though she was sorry for the poor little man, who ran so hard after the swift-footed creature that he fell down in the sand repeatedly.

Paulus wiped a hand over his forehead. "The day is hot." He patted Moriah's hand to get her full attention. "I will obtain refreshment, since our host has chosen not to offer any." He looked at Servius, who had turned his head to watch them. A veiled warning tinged Paulus's voice, and his jaw grew rigid. "You will be safe while I am gone, Moriah. I shall not be long."

"Of course." She almost asked to go with him but decided that would be childish. She was nervous and did not want him to leave, but she, too, was thirsty.

Almost as soon as Paulus disappeared from sight, Moriah heard Servius murmur to Flavia, "Leave us."

Eyes wide, Moriah watched as Flavia stood, pouting, and exited the box. Other than the two slaves attending Servius, Moriah was alone with the man. Regretting her decision not to ask Paulus if she could go with him, she clenched her hands in her lap. Out of the corner of her eye, she noticed Servius's gaze slowly travel over her face and down her form, then up again.

"The sun grows hot," he said, his voice silky. "Come. Sit beside me and share my shade. Such flawless skin as yours must be protected."

She tried to swallow, but her mouth was dry. "I am well. It is not so hot—not really." The trickle of perspiration on her upper lip belied her words.

Servius shifted and bent sideways, holding out his golden chalice. "Try some, Moriah. It is some of the finest wine in the empire. I see that you thirst. Do not tell me it is not so."

Moriah glanced at him. The look in his eyes bordered on irritation, and she knew it would not be wise to deny him a second time. She reached for the goblet, avoiding contact with his fingers. Uncomfortably aware that his gaze continued to rest on her, Moriah stared into the crimson liquid. She wondered if it was drugged with myrrh, as Flavia had told her was sometimes the case. She pretended to take a sip, being careful not to let the liquid even touch her lips, then handed the goblet back to him.

Instead of taking it, his hands covered hers, trapping them against the cool metal. Startled, her gaze snapped to his. Strong desire fiiled his eyes, a look that even one as inexperienced as she could not miss. Her heart raced with fear.

The laughter faded and the trumpets blared. The sudden piercing sound caused Servius to drop his hands away from hers and take back the goblet. Relieved, Moriah again focused her attention below, promising herself she would not look his way again. She hoped Paulus would soon return.

Young men entered the arena from all sides and began to fight with wooden swords. Their skill was evident as weapons crashed repeatedly against each other. Yet after a short time,

the crowd seemed bored. Some ignored the spectacle altogether and engaged in talk with those around them.
Throughout the mock battle, Moriah could feel Servius's gaze
on her. It was all she could do not to flee the box and search
out her cousin.

Much to her relief, Paulus returned. His expression was
stern. "Where's Flavia?" he asked her, his eyes cutting to
Servius and narrowing.

Moriah shrugged and gave a slight smile, hoping to lighten
his mood. Servius had frightened her, it was true, but nothing
had happened, and Moriah could sense Paulus was ready for
a fight.

"Why do they battle with wooden swords?" she asked, hoping to divert his mind to a topic that would interest him.

The corners of his lips turned upward in mockery, showing
her she had not fooled him one bit. "The *lusorii* fight to rouse
the people and warm their blood to prepare them for the real
fighting. However, they are far from doing so today. I sincerely doubt they could excite a small child." Paulus jeered at
the men, as others in the crowd were also doing.

Moriah was surprised. She thought they fought well.

As she watched, one of the men nearby swiftly raised his
wooden sword and brought it down hard on his opponent's
head. The victim slumped to the pale sand, and the crowd's
insulting jeers turned to cheering.

"How unusual," Paulus said, his tone mildly interested.
"The *lusorii* fight bloodless battles. Perhaps the combatant
was fearful for his life, due to the crowd's negative reaction,
or perhaps he held a grudge against his opponent. It does
prove an interesting twist to the games."

Moriah sensed Paulus turn his head her way, yet she could
do nothing but stare at the man's prone form. Was he truly
dead?

Paulus let out a mild oath and laid his hand over hers.
Feeling as though she were an unwilling participant in a night-
mare, Moriah looked at him.

"Forgive me for speaking so bluntly," he said. "I fear that due to my position as a Roman soldier, as well as having witnessed hundreds of games, I am accustomed to seeing men wounded or killed, and the sight of it no longer fazes me. We can go if you prefer, Moriah. Uncle need never know you left the circus early."

At that moment Flavia returned, demanding to know what she had missed. In a few curt words, Servius told her about the unusual fight between the two *lusorii,* and she grumbled, obviously disappointed not to have witnessed the spectacle.

Moriah would have liked nothing better than to leave this horrible place. Yet if she did, Flavia would tell her father, who in turn would tell Moriah's father, and she would never hear the end of it. She would be a disgrace to her father in his friends' eyes, as well as a disobedient daughter.

"I am well." Moriah offered Paulus a trembling smile. "We can stay."

He snorted in frustration, obviously not believing her stilted words, and offered her the wineskin he purchased. When she shook her head, he pushed it her way. "It is honeyed water. I know you dislike strong wine."

Grateful, she accepted it and took a drink. Cool and refreshing, the water came through the aqueducts and snow-covered Alban Hills beyond Rome and was sweetened with wild honey.

"Look, Moriah," Paulus said. "He lives."

Relieved, she focused on the arena. Two *lusorii* aided the wounded man to the gates, one on each side of him. Suddenly Moriah tensed.

A fair-haired man, strongly resembling Aidan, entered the arena close to the emperor's box. He wore no more than a loincloth and carried a spear. His muscled body glistened. A pack of vicious Molossian dogs was let loose, obviously starved, judging from the way the outline of their bones protruded through their fur. Moriah dug her fingernails deep into her thigh. She leaned forward, wishing she could do something to stop the madness. That could have been Aidan out there!

Yellow fangs bared, the animals attacked the man, who fought valiantly, killing two. A third large beast leaped onto him, sinking its teeth into his shoulder and bringing the man to his knees. Still he fought, to the obvious surprise of the crowd, and killed every wild dog there in a great show of skill and courage. Bloodied, his chest heaving, the man stood tall and turned to the emperor, awaiting his fate.

Moriah released the breath she was holding. Tasting blood, she became conscious of the fact that she'd bitten through the skin of her inner lip. She watched the cheering crowd stand and extend their hands with thumbs pointing in the air. *"Mitte! Mitte!"* they cried.

"A sign for mercy," Paulus told Moriah as he stood, pushing his thumb in the air, and she did the same. All eyes turned toward the emperor.

He hesitated, looking at the crowd around him, then gave the mercy sign. Unaided, the fair-haired man limped through the iron gates while the people cheered him with a deafening roar that shook the arena.

An intermission followed. Servius's slaves offered the guests a platter of fruit and various delicacies. Merely staring at the ripe offerings made Moriah's stomach churn, and she shook her head. Soon those who left the circus for intermission returned to their seats. Once Nero entered his podium with his aides, the trumpets blared.

Moriah tightly clutched the wineskin of honeyed water, realizing the death matches were about to begin. She had no need for Paulus to tell her so; she could see it written on every face in the crowd. Men and women craned their necks, eagerly looking toward the gates from which the gladiators emerged.

Each pair of warriors had a *lanista* to oversee their combat. Remembering former talks with Flavia, Moriah was able to pick out the trainers easily. The men were dressed in tunics and bore long rods, while the gladiators wore armor and shorter tunics. Paulus explained in an undertone to Moriah that of the pair of gladiators fighting closest to them, one was a *retiarius,* another a *secutor*—meaningless words to her. All she knew was that in minutes one man would be left standing, the other possibly dead. And after that? What happened to a man after he died? Did he cease to exist? Did he turn into an animal or other being as many believed? Or was there an afterlife—a heaven and hell—such as Deborah often spoke of?

Strangely unable to tear her gaze away from the horrible spectacle being played out on the sand, Moriah watched the two men closest to her fight one another in fierce combat. With each thrust and hit of the sword or trident, the crowd cheered and Moriah winced, her stomach clenching. After a time, when one man fell to his knees after being hopelessly caught in the weighted net of the other man, the crowd began to boo and scream in frenzy, *"Jugula! Jugula!"* Their thumbs turned downward.

In a plea for mercy, the wounded man on the ground lifted his arm toward the emperor's box. His winning opponent looked toward the emperor, as did Moriah. Nero raised his hand and extended his thumb downward. The victor turned and plunged his trident through the net, whereby the crowd began to cheer and call out the name of the winning gladiator. Moriah was certain she would be sick as she watched the defeated man's lifeblood pool onto the white sand.

Clapping a hand over her mouth, she shot up and fled the box. She hurried to the passageway, not caring what people thought of her behavior, not caring that they probably thought her less than a true daughter of Rome.

At the exit, she felt Paulus's firm hold on her elbow and was grateful for his support. Yet once she made it outside the high walls of the Circus Maximus, gratitude turned to embarrassment as her stomach began to empty itself of its contents.

Paulus clasped her shoulders and held her up, while she doubled over in agony. "Poor thing," she heard the sympathetic voice of an older woman say nearby. "I reacted the same when I saw my first kill years ago. She'll grow accustomed to it. I did."

The well-meaning words made Moriah feel worse instead of better. Trembling, she wiped the back of one shaky hand over her mouth, then faced her cousin. "Please, Paulus, take me away from this place of death," she whispered.

He gave her the wineskin of honeyed water and assisted her to his chariot. Grateful, she took a long drink of the cool liquid and forced herself to relax, feeling her stomach clench again at the thought of what she had seen.

Paulus drove the chariot down the narrow streets crowded with every type of humanity, from slave-borne litters carrying the wealthy, to the occasional beggar who stood on the fringes of the road, entreating those who passed by for alms. Had Moriah felt better, she would have suggested Paulus stop and give each man a coin. All she wanted now was to put as much distance between herself and the circus as possible. Even from this distance, she could hear the rise and ebb of the crowd's roar. Wishing her hands were free to clap over her ears, Moriah gripped the wineskin more tightly.

༚

Paulus stopped the chariot near a sumptuous garden. Peach and plum trees were among the fruit trees growing in the vast area, as well as tall and stately cypresses lining the paths.

"Citizens often take advantage of these grounds during the day," Paulus said. "I suspect this afternoon, however, we will have the place to ourselves, due to the games."

They walked along the pathway in the peaceful shade offered by boughs of overhanging limbs. Moriah allowed the beauty of her surroundings to soothe her spirit. Brilliantly colored flowers—roses, anemones, and irises—vied for attention along the ground and in the bushes. Marble statues dotted the area, some of which graced sparkling fountains.

Paulus was right. Except for a couple entwined in one another's arms under the shade of a flowering tree, the gardens were deserted. Hearing Paulus and Moriah approach, the lovers broke apart, as though guilty. Seeing it was only strangers who'd come upon them and not someone they knew, they embraced again.

Paulus led Moriah down a more secluded path, until they came to a bench near a statue of Ceres, goddess of agriculture. "Let us rest here," he suggested.

Grateful for the privacy, Moriah nodded. She had not spoken since they left the circus, and now she eyed her cousin, her heart troubled. "Are you angry with me, Paulus?"

Judging from his surprised reaction, it was the last thing he'd expected her to say. "Angry? Why should I be angry with you?"

Her gaze lowered to her lap. "Because of my embarrassing conduct. Because of my cowardice at the arena. I doubt a true daughter of Rome would have acted in such a disgraceful manner."

Paulus took a place beside her and grabbed her shoulders. "Do you honestly believe I think you any less a daughter of Rome because you could not stomach the bloodshed you were forced to watch?"

She did not answer.

"No, Moriah. I think you a queen among women. You stand out—a prized rose in a field of common wildflowers. I've always thought so. I was not jesting when I told you that Venus could not hold a candle to your loveliness. Perhaps you are a goddess sent to earth in the guise of a mortal to show me a glimpse of beauty in its purest form—to give me hope that such things as innocence and sweetness do exist in a world gone mad."

After his low, heartfelt avowal, he turned her face upward with a finger beneath her chin and made her look at him. She felt faint and a little frightened with the knowledge that he would kiss her—her first kiss. Yet when his lips touched hers, Moriah had the oddest sense of something being. . .wrong. There was no other explanation for the stilted feeling his kiss produced. He, too, must have felt it, for he drew back and studied her, his eyes confused.

To cover the awkward moment, Moriah quickly spoke. "I have something I wish to ask you, Paulus. Something that has troubled me since I overheard you and Father argue in the *bibliotheca* five nights ago."

His jaw grew rigid. "You heard our conversation?"

She averted her gaze. "Yes, though I did not hear all that was said. I know I should not have listened—but when I heard my name mentioned, I simply could not leave."

Again, he placed his finger beneath her chin and tipped her face, this time as though she were a child. "You know what happened in the Greek tale of Pandora when she insisted on looking into the forbidden box. Curiosity can be a dangerous thing, little dove."

Relieved he had slipped into the familiar role of acting as an older brother, she relaxed and offered him a faint smile. "I am well aware of that. Unfortunately, as you well know, curiosity has been one of my greatest evils to conquer. Even so, I wish to question you regarding something Father said."

A guarded look came into his eyes, and he dropped his hand away from her face. "I cannot promise I will answer. But, of course, you may ask."

She swallowed hard. "Is Marcus Seneca your true father?"

His eyes widened in shock. Evidently she had surprised him once again. "Of course. Why would you ask such a thing?"

Tears stung Moriah's eyes, and she hastily blinked them back. She had pondered the men's conversation for days and arrived at two conclusions. Paulus had just nullified one of them. Though she wanted to plead with him to tell her the truth, no matter what it revealed, her manner remained poised.

"Tell me then, Paulus, who are my true parents?"

A colorful bird began a low-pitched trill from a nearby fruit tree. Ignoring Moriah's question, Paulus rose from the bench and strode toward the tree. He plucked a ripe peach from its branches and offered it to Moriah, but she only shook her head.

"Please, tell me the truth," she said very quietly. "I think I have a right to know."

Paulus clenched the rosy-golden morsel in his hand until the juice trickled between his fingers. With a look of disgust, he threw the peach to the ground and wiped his sticky hand down the side of his tunic. "Yes. You deserve to know. Moreover, it is not right that Uncle never told you." He shook his head. "Yet neither is it my place to reveal the truth, no matter how unjust his decision may be."

Moriah rose from the bench and lifted her hands in supplication. "What can it matter now that I know? Surely it is better to know the truth in its entirety than to know only in part and arrive at conclusions that may not be valid? Please, Paulus. I must know what the mystery is. I cannot explain it, for I do not understand it myself, but until I learn everything, I cannot feel whole again."

Paulus briefly closed his eyes, then he reached for another peach and bit into its fuzzy skin. "Very well, Moriah. You always were able to wheedle your way where I was concerned, ever since you were old enough to walk."

She felt her cheeks warm at his low words but nodded for him to go on.

"Your father was a retired Roman tribune by the name of Rexus Caspus. As a child I looked up to him and have often tried to emulate him in my life as a soldier. Your mother—Helena—was from Corinth, though your father met her here in Rome. When he retired, they married, and you were born a year later."

Something in his somber attitude alerted Moriah that there was more to this than he was saying. "I want to know everything, Paulus."

He looked away to the peach tree and clenched his hands. "Your father and mother were arrested during Caligula's reign and pronounced guilty."

"Guilty?" she whispered. "Why? What did they do?"

He shook his head in disgust. "There were spies in the empire then, as I suspect there are now. Someone with the ear of the emperor told him there was a well-loved citizen of

Rome who was a traitor."

"My father was a traitor?" Moriah could not keep the horror from her voice.

Paulus looked at her. "I never believed him to be," he quickly said, "and still do not. Rexus Caspus had a heart for Rome and was a loyal and honored soldier, respected and loved by the people. He had favor in the eyes of the emperor Tiberius, as well."

"Then for what reason. . .I mean surely if he were as well respected as you imply, the words spoken against him would have counted for nothing. Why did Caligula not believe my father's innocence? You told me my father found favor with the empire."

Paulus grimaced and again looked away. "Caligula was mad, believing himself to be a god—the brother of Jupiter— and demanding worship. There were many who were jealous of the favor your father had gained and wanted to be rid of him, though I still am uncertain who turned him in. I was only fourteen at the time."

"Turned him in?" Moriah shook her head, baffled. "What is it you are keeping from me, Paulus? Why was my father considered a traitor?"

The dark eyes he turned her way were full of sympathy. "Your parents were of the religious sect known as Christians, Moriah. When Caspus and Helena refused to renounce their faith and bow down and worship Caligula as a god, Caligula had them both beheaded."

Moriah sank to the bench, sudden weakness overcoming her. "Beheaded," she whispered.

Paulus rushed to her side. "I should not have told you," he said, sounding angry with himself.

"No. I asked and am grateful to know. And yet I am shocked to learn my parents could have belonged to such a terrible order. And that they died for their beliefs as well."

Paulus seemed to consider her words. "Moriah, I don't know what you've been told concerning these Christians. I myself have heard alarming things about them, though I'm ignorant of their practices. But I knew your father and mother. They were good people. When Caspus joined the Christians, he became a different person, though I am uncertain of how to explain this. Tribune Caspus had always been just, and the people looked up to him, even before his conversion. But afterward he was. . .more settled, gentle even, though he was in no way considered a coward."

Moriah didn't feel convinced, though she was pleased to hear that her true parents had possessed a few admirable traits.

"Moriah, I assure you, neither he nor your mother poisoned wells, killed babies, or worshiped a donkey's head. I would stake my life on it." His eyes flamed with sincerity. "I am not certain how such rumors started, but I feel it might have been instigated by the Jews. For some reason they despise the Christians, though they both worship the same God. I believe it is because of this Jesus, whom they call the *Christus*—the Messiah—that their views differ."

"You seem to know much about the subject," Moriah said quietly.

Paulus gave her a mocking smile. "Only what I remember your father telling me. He was in Jerusalem, in Judea, during the time Jesus walked the earth. When Jesus was executed, your father was in charge of the group of soldiers who scourged Him. Caspus told me he fashioned a crown of thorns to put on Jesus' head—since Jesus called Himself a king—and Caspus thought Him a madman at the time.

"Later, at the foot of the cross, Caspus heard Jesus call out to His Father to forgive all those who had harmed Him. Your father had never heard anything like it, nor had he seen anything like what happened afterward. The sky grew dark as night, though it was midday, and the earth shook and broke apart. He told me that later people claimed their departed loved ones had risen from their graves. And many more claimed the dead man, Jesus, rose from the dead on the third day after he was killed and was seen by hundreds of others in different parts of the region before disappearing into the clouds forty days later." Paulus shook his head, his eyes mirroring the incredulity Moriah felt.

She gasped. *"Rose from the dead?"*

"That is what Caspus said, though I find it hard to believe as well. Such occurrences do not happen. Yet your father was never one to speak a falsehood."

Moriah tried to absorb the fantastic things Paulus told her, but she could not grasp them. "And my father? How did he become a Christian if he was the one responsible for this man Jesus' death?"

"Caspus heard one of Jesus' followers—an apostle called Peter—talk in the marketplace weeks later and saw him perform the same miracles Jesus had done—healing the sick, the blind, and the lame. After speaking with Peter, Caspus told me it was then that he believed. All I know for a certainty is this: Caspus returned to Rome a different man from the one who left."

Stunned, Moriah could find no reply.

The expression on Paulus's face softened, and he covered her hand with his. "Perhaps it is time we return to the house. We can talk more on this later."

Her mind a confusing clamor of thoughts, Moriah managed a nod. There was only one person she desperately wanted to speak with—soon—when she could sort all this out and think clearly. She was convinced only Aidan could answer her unspoken questions.

four

Moriah wandered through the *peristylium,* seeing little, feeling nothing. Her mind constantly replayed the conversation between herself and Paulus in the gardens. The revelation of her true heritage seemed like some fantastic and horrible dream.

Her green-eyed Abyssinian cat, which Paulus had secured in Egypt and brought to her as a gift when she turned eleven, slunk out from behind a stone statue of Diana and rubbed silky fur against her legs. In her little-girl wisdom, Moriah had named her pet for the emperor who ruled during that time.

"Claudius! Where have you been?" Moriah crooned, bending over to pick up the sleek, fat animal. Obviously there was no lack of mice in the vicinity. She buried her face in Claudius's golden brown fur and promptly sneezed, alarming him. He jumped from her arms and onto the tiles. Yet he did not dart away, instead pattering beside Moriah as she strolled toward the garden at the rear of the house.

Cat hairs clung to her *stola,* but she did not mind. It was nice to have companionship—even if it was only a cat's. Lydia was sick with a fever, and Deborah had retired to her room for the evening, complaining of a headache. Flavia had avoided Moriah since the games, obviously still perturbed with her early departure from them. And Paulus was constantly busy since that day, involved with his duties in serving the emperor.

Reaching the arbor, Moriah stepped inside, half hoping to find Aidan. Of course, he wasn't there. Likely he was somewhere in the house, attending her father. Moriah sank to the bench, remembering her encounter here with Aidan a week ago. Had only one week passed since that night? It seemed much more than that.

Though Moriah was uncertain what her feelings were concerning the Christians—especially after learning her true parents were of that sect—she was intrigued with the little Aidan had told her on that special evening they conversed. And she wished to hear more. Closing her eyes, she settled back and listened to the lyrical, far-off notes of a nightingale.

Exactly where did she belong?

She wished to know more about former tribune Rexus Caspus and his wife, Helena—the woman who had given birth to her. Paulus had told her little about the woman. Only that she was Greek and was kind. Yet how had Helena and Rexus known Lydia and Clophelius? Now that Moriah knew the truth about her parentage and had come to accept it, she wanted answers. Answers for which she did not care to wait. Yet neither was she certain whom to ask.

She turned her gaze to the neatly trimmed bushes, and a memory surfaced from the mists of her mind. She had been a child playing in the courtyard near the fountain, plucking flowers from neat rows, tearing off petals and tossing them into the water. "Praise be to the Almighty God and to the Lord and Savior, Jesus Christ," the six-year-old Moriah repeated in a singsong voice as she skipped around the fountain, mimicking what she'd heard an old woman softly exclaim to another in the marketplace that morning.

Her father, Clophelius, was talking nearby with a friend. Angrily he turned on Moriah, wrested the remaining flowers from her pudgy little hands, and threw them to the ground. Eyes blazing with fury, he raised his hand as though to strike.

Moriah cowered, putting her crossed arms in front of her face. "Father—no!"

His expression uncertain, he lowered his hand, then turned on Deborah, spilling his wrath onto the young woman. He slapped her twice, demanding to know if she was the one responsible for teaching Moriah treason. Fearfully, the maidservant denied it.

After that incident, Moriah was rarely let out of the house

and was no longer allowed to accompany Deborah to the marketplace or to any of the other shops along the streets. Not until she was sixteen had Father given his permission for her to visit places other than the temples to which her mother occasionally forced her to go. By that time, Moriah preferred the restful beauty of the garden to the chaos of the noisy city, the one exception being her visits to the market with Deborah.

Perhaps there was something of the gentle Helena inside Moriah and that was why she was different from other Romans. A soft smile lifted her lips at the thought. She would not mind sharing the traits of such a woman. Yet one question invaded her mind, troubling her: Why had the secret of her heritage remained hidden from her all this time?

&

Once Aidan finished giving Clophelius a massage, firmly rubbing knotted muscles in his withered legs and flabby back that so often cramped and caused pain, his master dismissed him. Though Clophelius had his own muscular bodyguard who carried him from room to room, the master relied solely on Aidan for other services and seemed more at ease when he was in the vicinity.

Aidan bowed and exited the incense-laden room through clouds of red smoke, knowing from experience that his services would not be required again until morning. From his post by the entryway, Kryton, Clophelius's bodyguard, gave Aidan a scornful look. Aidan ignored the heavyset man and continued along the corridor. In the nine years Aidan had served Clophelius, the master had favored Aidan above his other household slaves, instilling envy in many of them. Often the master commended Aidan, even rewarding him with a few *sesterces* or a *denarius* from time to time. Aidan did not know why Clophelius treated him so well, but each day he thanked the Lord for favor.

As he entered the garden lit by the early evening sun, his thoughts turned to Moriah and their late-night talk in the arbor the previous week. Often he thought of his lady, envisioning her delicate features, recalling her melodic voice and the sweet aroma of her jasmine fragrance. Rueful, he shook his head as though to dispel the vision of her violet-blue eyes looking up at him. It could do no harm to dream.

Or could it?

Putting his hand to the slim trunk of a flowering oleander, Aidan stared at a nearby branch bearing numerous clusters of white flowers. *Oh God, why did You place me here? I am only a mortal, and Moriah is everything I desire in a woman. Deliver me from temptation, oh, Lord, my God—*

"Aidan."

He started at the sound of Deborah's curt voice and moved to face the Jewess. Her dark eyes were solemn, her mouth turned down at the corners. "We need to talk," she said, her gaze darting around the garden as if she were afraid of being overheard. "Walk with me and carry this, so no one will suspect us."

Curious, Aidan accepted the bronze pitcher she held out to him and matched his steps to hers.

"I know of your late-night sojourns in this garden," she murmured, her words clipped. "And they must stop."

A weed of alarm unfurled in Aidan's mind, but he quickly stomped it down. "It was you I heard that night."

"Yes, and if you value your life, you will cease such practices." She threw him a sideways glance. "You must not speak again of your faith to Moriah. It is a dangerous thing."

Aidan considered her warning. He knew he could trust Moriah; otherwise, he would have not spoken. "My lady has given me her word she'll not divulge my secret. I have no reason to doubt her."

Deborah stopped and whirled to face him, grabbing his arm as though she might shake him. "Don't be a fool, Aidan! Moriah has been raised a Roman and knows no other way. In the end, she will do what she's been taught is right. Yet it is not only for your sake that I tell you this."

Aidan lifted his brows. "Yes?" he prompted.

Her eyes glittered with warning. "Stay away from Moriah. You could only do her harm."

"I would never harm her," he argued, raising his voice, but Deborah gave a brisk shake of her head, halting his fervent denial.

She scanned the garden quickly, then returned her gaze to his. "That you are a Christian is enough to harm her. If not in body, then in spirit. The added fact that you remain a slave and she your mistress should be reason enough for you to keep your distance." Her fingers tightened around his arm and her nails dug into his flesh. "I will not see my lady harmed! Do you hear, Aidan? I would kill you before I allowed that to happen."

He regarded the stern countenance of the small woman in front of him. Fierce loyalty shone from her eyes and in every nuance of her expression. "Tell me, Deborah, if you despise me so greatly, why would you warn me to cease praying at the arbor? Why would you care if I were caught or not?"

Her features softened, and sadness filled her eyes. "I once knew others who were of your faith," she said quietly, "and it is to them I owe everything. Even my life."

"Then why. . . ?"

She gave another curt shake of her head, as though impatient with his questions. "We have said enough. I must go. Heed my words, Aidan. I do not speak them lightly."

Before he could respond, she plucked the pitcher from his grasp and hurried away.

಄

All afternoon Moriah was restless. When it came time for *cena* and Deborah informed her that neither her mother, who was ill, nor her father, who lay in heavy slumber, would partake of the evening meal, Moriah requested food be brought to her *cubiculum*. She disliked the idea of eating alone in the large, elegant *triclinium* and opted for her sunny terrace instead.

Two slaves strode toward her, bearing platters containing pigs' feet steeped in pickled wine, baked apples drenched in golden honey, delectable fresh fruits, and sweet wine cakes liberally sprinkled with dates and nuts. Spotting Deborah behind them, Moriah motioned her maid to take a place at the round table two more servants set before her.

"You must share *cena* with me tonight, Deborah." Moriah sank to the couch beside the table and reclined on her side, against the cushions. She turned to one of the women. "Bring another goblet."

"Yes, my lady," the girl said, bowing.

Deborah glanced at the main course, her expression doubtful. Moriah felt instant remorse. "Forgive me, Deborah. I forgot that your religion forbade such foods. Still, you can eat the wine cakes and fruit, can you not?"

"Yes, my lady." Deborah sank to the adjoining couch and accepted the goblet a slave handed her. She plucked a Persian peach from the heap of fruit on the bronze platter and took a small bite.

Pensive, Moriah studied her maidservant. Making a snap decision, Moriah dismissed all the other slaves, leaving her and Deborah alone. Sunlight streamed in through the lattice window, shedding diamond shapes of gold upon the terrace. A cooling wind blew through the openings and helped make the evening more tolerable.

"Deborah," Moriah said thoughtfully, selecting a wine cake from the tray. "Is it not true that the Jewish people and those who call themselves Christians worship the same God?"

Deborah's head jerked upward. Moriah kept her attention focused on the cake, trying to act as if the matter were of little interest to her and merely an attempt at conversation.

"It is true that we both worship the God of our father Abraham," Deborah said warily, "but the Christians also worship the teacher Jesus, claiming Him to be Messiah. In this we differ."

"So you have reason to believe this Jesus was not Messiah?" Moriah glanced at Deborah, noting her anxious expression and death grip on the rosy-golden fruit. Her ragged fingernails dug deeply into the thin skin. "Be at peace, Deborah. I do not question to bring you harm. I am merely curious about this religion."

"Might I ask from where this curiosity stems?"

Moriah averted her gaze to the swirled design carved onto the sides of the table. The words were still difficult to say. "My true father, though he was a well-loved Roman citizen and loyal to the empire, believed Jesus was the Christ to the point of dying for this belief. My true mother did as well. I have discovered I am the *adopted* daughter of Clophelius Dinoculus."

Deborah released a long sigh fraught with relief. "Praise be to the Most High God," she whispered emphatically. "At last you know."

Startled, Moriah stared at her maid, not expecting such a reaction. Surprise—definitely. Or shock or disbelief. Yet none of those emotions were evident on the dusky face smiling at her from across the table.

"What do you know of this?" A tremor filled Moriah's voice. "Tell me, Deborah."

"It was I who brought you to this house almost twenty-three years ago when you were but an infant," the woman admitted softly.

Moriah gasped. "You knew my parents?"

"Yes." Deborah's expression grew pensive as though she were remembering. "After my parents died in my birthplace of Jerusalem, the innkeeper next door forced me into servitude. Later, when I was ten years of age, he sold me to slavers on a ship bound for Rome. Helena bought me and treated me with kindness during the two years I served her and your father."

Moriah leaned forward in excitement, almost overturning her goblet. "Tell me everything you remember about them."

"As you wish, my lady. Now that you know the truth, I can see no harm in it."

Moriah avidly listened while Deborah recounted much of what Paulus already had told her, though she added other information as well. Moriah learned her parents changed when they converted to the Faith and freed their slaves, afterward moving to an *insulae* along the Trans-Tiber, where many plebeians lived. Her mother, Helena, made and sold fine cloth. She often visited the sick and the dying, offering words of encouragement and bringing food. Due to his military background, former tribune Rexus Caspus became a strong helper to the Christians, interfering when trouble arose between them and any Roman soldiers who enjoyed mocking the new religious sect.

"But your father had to keep his true faith from being discovered in order to do this," Deborah explained. She lowered her gaze to her lap. "Afterward, it was discovered that someone—though it was never known who—told Caligula that Caspus was a traitor to Rome and was suspected of being a Christian. Late one night while the household lie sleeping, Praetorian soldiers came to the *insulae* and arrested your father and mother, taking them to the palace. I only just managed to escape with you. I was so frightened. I was certain they would capture and kill us both. In my haste, I left my sandals behind, and my feet were bleeding by the time I arrived. I came here, to the house of Dinoculus, as your mother had once told me to do should danger ever arise."

Visibly shaken by the memory, Deborah let her eyelids slide shut. "Days later—in the emperor's private arena at Caligula's birthday celebration—your father and mother were both beheaded as traitors to the Roman Empire."

Moriah stared into the distance. The food had long been forgotten, and a heavy silence cloaked the balcony, though the streets below were boisterous with activity.

"I find it curious," Moriah said in a small voice. "If this Jesus was not the Messiah as the Christians claim, then why are so many willing to give up everything they have and even die for their faith?"

Deborah's brows drew together. "I, too, have wondered. Especially after having heard of the love and mercy your parents showed others—even when they were shown neither." Her voice wavered with emotion. Dark eyes swimming with tears, she steadily regarded Moriah. "You see, before they were killed, your father and mother publicly forgave their executioners."

Stunned, Moriah inhaled swiftly, tears forming in her own eyes. Who were these people—these Christians? And what gave them the ability to do such things?

"My father was a priest from the house of Levi," Deborah continued. "He warned me long ago to beware of false prophets. That when Messiah came, He would come with many armies and be a strong leader who would deliver His people from Roman captivity.

"Yet this Jesus the Christians worship died on a cross a despised criminal. I remember your father saying that He offered no resistance but went willingly. That doesn't sound like a leader to me. And yet, when I see the love displayed by these people—even toward their enemies—I think, who but God could make such a thing possible?" Deborah shook her head as though she had no answers.

"I see."

Moriah stared at one of the golden diamonds of sunlight on the wall, her thoughts a maelstrom of confusion. Deborah reached across the table and wrapped strong fingers around Moriah's wrist, startling her mistress into meeting her gaze.

"No matter about this Jesus," Deborah said fiercely. "I know you have a purpose for being here, my lady. Lydia told me on the evening that I brought you to this house that the goddess Juno had finally blessed her with a child. Yet I know differently—as did your true mother. The Most High God was the One who brought you to this place of refuge and has continued to keep you safe—as He did with Moses—until the time comes when He will use you for His divine plan. Helena once told me she knew that God had a special purpose for you, that He shared this with her while she was in prayer."

Deborah's gaze was mesmerizing as she said with confidence, "I know, through listening to the Holy Scriptures, that the Most High does talk with a chosen few of His people.

Your mother was beautiful in both form and spirit. I do not doubt her word; I believe God truly spoke to her."

Ill at ease, Moriah snatched her hand away from Deborah's strong grip, uncertain what to say, uncertain what it was that her maid wanted her to say. Did she expect Moriah to embrace such a disclosure with eagerness? Rather, the words frightened her. Exactly what did this God of her mother's want from her?

A shadow descended over Deborah's eyes, and she quickly rose to her feet, averting her gaze. "My lady, if there's nothing else, I have duties to which I must attend."

"Of course. You may go." Moriah usually enjoyed Deborah's company, but now she preferred that the woman leave her alone.

Once Deborah hastened away, Moriah somberly stared out over the bustling city of Rome. Time passed, evident by the gradual shifting rays of the setting sun across the table. She remained lost in a time she knew nothing about, a time that took place before she was born.

❧

Moriah watched the flickering shadows on the ceiling, made discernable by the moon that flooded her terrace with dim light. Thin wavy lines overhead seemed to slither, and she imagined them to be serpents.

Memory of a story Deborah once sang to her about a man named Adam and a woman named Eve came to mind. A cunning serpent in their garden tricked them, telling the couple they could become like gods if they ate the forbidden fruit. Had such a serpent tricked the emperor Caligula and convinced him that he was a god and not a mere mortal? If Adam had resisted and put his heel on the serpent's head, killing it so that it could not later trick Caligula, would her parents be alive today?

Blowing out an impatient breath, Moriah turned on her side. From where did these questions come? No serpent could live for centuries—unless it was not a true serpent at all but an immortal being disguised as a serpent.

She squeezed her eyes shut and tried not to think. Outside, a bird began to chirp merrily as though it did not realize the sky was dark. Perhaps it was blind. Was there such a thing as blind birds? Moriah wondered how her childhood tutor Malchus would have responded to such a question. He often reprimanded her about her continual use of them and told her it was not a girl's place to question, only to accept what was instructed of her first by her father and later by her husband.

Moriah sighed and opened her eyes. It was of no use. She could not sleep.

A breeze blew in through the lattices, gently disturbing the gauze curtain that shielded her bed, and beckoned her. She sat up and pulled the thin drape aside, answering the call.

Without summoning her maid for assistance, Moriah slipped on a *stola* lying nearby and hastily tied a cord around her waist. On bare feet, she padded along the corridor, thankful to see no one in the vicinity. Opening the door to the gardens, she noticed two things. The half moon sat low in the sky, evidence dawn would soon be upon them, and the torches placed along the pathways were unlit, so the way was dim.

Moriah quietly made her way to the arbor. She glanced inside the structure but found it empty. Not sure what propelled her to walk farther, she continued down the pathway along the far wall, past sculpted bushes and fir trees.

Hearing footsteps softly crunch nearby, she stopped in shock. As she watched, the door in the high garden wall leading to the outside creaked open. Her heart sped up and her eyes widened with fright. A large, hooded figure—obviously a man—crept into the garden and closed the door behind him. A thief? An assassin?

Not sure if she should call for Jacabar or try to slip away unnoticed, then make a frantic run for it and seek help, Moriah did neither. Her feet seemed to have become rooted to the ground like that of the surrounding trees. The inside of her mouth went dry as bark. She wanted to scream, but no sound would issue forth.

The cloaked figure took a few steps in her direction and stopped, obviously having spotted her. Lifting his arms, he pulled the dark mantle from his head, revealing long hair that shone pale in the moonlight. "My lady?"

Moriah almost fainted with relief. "Aidan," she breathed, her hand going to a tree trunk for support. Her limbs felt shaky, and she inhaled a deep lungful of air, feeling as though she might collapse.

Evidently realizing her situation, he closed the distance and put a supportive hand to her upper arm; she leaned her forehead against his chest until she felt more stable. Yet being so close to the warmth of his muscular body, which had an appealing musky smell that was all Aidan's, produced the opposite effect. Moriah took a shaky step away, confused by the sudden onslaught of unfamiliar feelings.

Instantly Aidan released her. "I'm sorry to have frightened you, my lady. I'll go." He moved in the opposite direction.

"No—don't leave!" Moriah put a hand on his cloaked arm to stop him. "I wish to speak with you in the arbor. I have for some time."

He seemed taken aback by her request but followed her to the small structure. She sank to the bench. He remained standing, and she motioned to the empty space beside her.

"Please, Aidan. Sit. . .so that I do not have to crane my neck to look up at you," she added, hoping to ease any discomfort he might feel at the idea of sitting in her presence.

He hesitated, then took a seat on the ground. Because he was in shadows, Moriah was unable to tell if he looked directly at her or not. Why it mattered to her so strongly, she didn't know.

"I am curious about your God," she began. "I want to know more about Him and your practices, as well."

There was a long pause, as though he were struggling with some inner conflict. "I would be happy to tell you all I know, my lady, if you are truly interested." His words were hesitant. "However, I cannot help but wonder. Does this request stem from a genuine desire to know the Truth? Or is it an idle curiosity hatched from boredom, which in turn could prove dangerous to followers of the Way?"

"You dare question me?" she asked in shocked surprise.

"In this matter, I can do no less. Forgive me, my lady, but there are other lives at stake, as well as my own."

Moriah studied his shadowed shape. For a slave to question his mistress was regarded as insolence and often brought instant punishment. Yet she knew she would never give the order to have any of their household slaves beaten, especially Aidan, whom she considered less a slave than the others.

"Be at peace, Aidan. I mean you no harm, as I have told you before. Nor do I wish to endanger your friends. I've been curious since last we talked. Now, more so than ever."

Her gaze dropped to the dim outline of her bare toes peeking from beneath the hem of her *stola*. "Recently, I discovered I am adopted. Both of my parents were Roman citizens, as well as Christians, and it is my belief that if I could learn something of their faith, I might understand why they did what they did. They are both dead," she added in a hushed voice. "Executed, I am told."

"I am sorry, my lady."

The sympathy gently ringing in his voice assured Moriah that he was sincere. She lifted her gaze to his shadowed face. "Please, Aidan, tell me all that you know."

He studied her delicate features lit by the moon's gentle glow, her form in the pale yellow *stola,* her luxurious dark hair streaming past her waist—and swallowed hard. He knew she could not see him where he sat in the dark; nevertheless, he forced himself to look away.

Uncertain how to begin, he told her about the old prophecies of the Jews being fulfilled in the man called Jesus. He repeated all he had learned about Jesus' life, His teachings, His healings and miracles, His death and resurrection. As Aidan relayed the gospel message, a fire burned within, and he grew excited, his words gaining momentum, though he was careful not to raise his voice to the tone he normally used when speaking.

Much later, he relaxed against the arbor's wall, wishing for a drink to refresh his parched throat. "I have told you all I know, my lady, all I have heard from the teachings of the apostle Peter. He walked with the Master—" Aidan broke off, surprised when she abruptly leaned forward and clutched his shoulder.

"He is in Rome? This man Peter?" Moriah leaned closer until he breathed in her sweet jasmine scent. Her eyes intently stared into his, and he found he could not look away even had he wanted to. "You were with him earlier, were you not? That is where you were tonight. With Peter and the others?"

Aidan hesitated. Leaving the house without permission, especially at night, was cause for severe punishment. Yet he would not lie to his lady.

"Aidan?"

"Yes," he admitted. "I was with Peter and the others."

Her grip tightened on his shoulder, though Aidan doubted she realized it. "Take me to him."

He inhaled swiftly at her excited words. "It would not be safe to do so, my lady. Dawn is on the horizon, and the way is far. Near the *Via Salaria*. I am not even certain he would still be at the place where we met."

"Where is this place?" she insisted.

He was quiet a moment. "In *koimeterion*."

"Koimeterion?"

"The catacombs."

Moriah's eyes widened. "The place of the dead?" she whispered. "Where the Jews keep their departed?"

"Yes, my lady. Though the message the apostle speaks is one of life."

Moriah bit her lip, uncertain. Why would the Christians meet in such a morbid place, outside city walls, unless the rumors about them were true? Perhaps they did perform vile rituals and used the black of night for their cloak of secrecy.

"Many in Rome despise the Way, the Christian teaching, though they know nothing of its principles," Aidan said into the silence as though he had read her mind. "For this reason, some have chosen not to gather in public, but instead prefer to hide and worship in seclusion. They feel the situation will only worsen and are fearful that Nero might incline his ear to fables and one day prohibit Christianity. Already some of our people have been beaten or abused in other ways by the empire as well as by anyone who bears hatred toward us, the numbers of which are many."

"Is it true that your religion teaches treason?" Her soft-spoken question bordered on fear.

"No, my lady. The King and kingdom we look forward to are not of this world. Even the Master Himself said to 'render to Caesar what is Caesar's and to God what is God's.' We have no wish to overthrow the government or to rally against it. Our teachings are based on love for our fellow men, even our enemies. Love is the only possible weapon to combat the evil in the world today."

Moriah listened to him, fascinated. "Who are you, Aidan?" she said softly to herself in wonder, giving voice to the question that had plagued her for years. Realizing the words had slipped from her mouth of their own accord and noting his surprised reaction, she hastened to add, "You do not act like any slave I have known, nor do you talk like one. You seem highly educated. I know you are from Britain. Yet I know little else about you."

During their conversation the night sky had lightened, and bold streaks of vermilion painted the eastern horizon. A soft rosy hue filled the arbor, making his startled face seem to glow. Moriah's heart skipped a beat when she realized his dark blue eyes were looking directly into hers.

As if he, too, had become aware of the fact, Aidan quickly averted his gaze to the wall beside them. "My grandfather was chieftain of our tribe before the Romans conquered our village. I was twelve summers when my people rose up in revolt, but the Romans were too numerous and powerful, killing most, making slaves and gladiators of the rest. I was taken aboard a slave ship, then sold to Crispus Laurentius, a scholar in Rome. He trained me as his apprentice and taught me to read and write in both Arabic and Greek. When he died of sickness three years later, again I was put on the auction block, where Hermes purchased me for the master."

Moriah shook her head in wonder. "And how did you come to be a Christian?"

"While I was in the house of Laurentius, I met another slave there. I was full of bitterness at the time—angry that all my family had been killed during the bloody battle with the Romans. Naoni's story was similar to mine, but her behavior was opposite. I could not understand how she could forgive those who abused her and killed her family. It was she who told me about the Way." A slight smile lifted the corners of his mouth.

Moriah fidgeted with the skirt of her *stola,* uncomfortable by his mention of Naoni. What had she been to him? By the look softening his features, she must have been special.

"And what happened to the slave, this Naoni?" she asked, not certain she really wanted to know but unable to stop the question from springing forth.

"She, too, was sold, though I know not where. One day, I intend to find her."

Moriah closed her eyes at the determination in his voice. Suddenly she was weary. She had been awake the entire night, and dawn was on the horizon. A mighty torrent of shame crashed through her. She could easily take to her bed and sleep into the afternoon if she so desired. Yet Aidan was a slave and incapable of engaging in such luxury.

"Aidan, forgive me."

"My lady?" His words were filled with shocked confusion.

"If it had not been for me, you could have obtained at least a few hours' rest. But now the day has begun," she explained, lifting her head to look at him.

This time it was Moriah who was startled by the soft look that filled his eyes. Eyes that at this moment were staring steadily into hers. And this time he did not turn away.

"It will not be the first night I have gone without sleep in this house," Aidan said quietly. His words seemed to hold deeper meaning as he continued to stare, and Moriah found she could barely draw breath. "I should return to my quarters before Hermes comes looking for me," he added.

She nodded, unable to speak. Before he moved three steps from the arbor, she found her voice again. "Aidan!" She slid off the bench and closed the short distance between them.

"My lady?"

"I wish to go with you to the next meeting." Her words came out as more of a hesitant question rather than a direct order. She put a tentative hand to his bare arm. "Please, Aidan. It was Peter to whom my father spoke. My cousin tells me that Peter is responsible for my father converting to Christianity. I only wish to question the man and ask him more about my father."

A wide range of emotions flickered in Aidan's eyes before he focused on the arched door leading to the *peristylium*. "I will let you know the day and the hour," he replied, a catch in his voice. Turning, he hurriedly walked to the house.

five

Despite the ray of hope Moriah felt after her talk with Aidan, the weeks that followed scattered clouds of despair across her horizon.

Lydia was not recovering from her latest bout of illness, which had come upon her days ago. Along with the fever, she had started coughing up blood. A physician applied leeches, trying to bring her humors into balance, but the expression on his face was grim. Solemnly he informed Clophelius there was little else to be done.

As if that weren't upsetting enough, Flavia unexpectedly appeared at the house one afternoon, having forgiven Moriah for her "infantile" and "embarrassing" behavior at the games. Once more, Flavia was the harbinger of alarming news, making Moriah apprehensive.

"But I do not wish to attend his banquet, Flavia. You must decline the invitation for me."

The blond pouted. "Servius expressly asked for you to be there. It is quite an honor, Moriah, him singling you out in such a manner. You cannot refuse. He is a powerful person, remember, as is my father."

Flavia's smooth words sounded like a threat, and surprised, Moriah sharply studied the woman. Her cat-green eyes looked back without wavering, and she lifted her brow in question. Moriah's gaze dropped to her lap.

"Perhaps I should speak to your father," Flavia mused.

"No. You needn't bother. I will talk to him."

What a horrible turn of fate! Only this morning, Aidan had informed Moriah that the Christians would be meeting in two nights, in someone's home this time. The same night as the banquet Servius was giving at his home, to which Flavia

insisted Moriah must go. And Moriah had told Aidan she
would go with him.

Though she harbored grave doubts about his faith, Moriah
wished to attend the meeting and see for herself if the shock-
ing rumors were true. Certainly they must be false if Aidan
was a Christian. Moriah could not imagine him partaking of
such atrocities. She hoped that Clophelius would agree with
her decision to decline the invitation Servius Antonus sent
through Flavia. After all, Lydia was quite ill.

As Flavia chattered about her latest affair, Moriah thought
about the parents who had raised her. Out of respect, she
continued to verbally address them as Mother and Father.
However, in her thoughts these past weeks, they ceased being
that, now that she knew she did not truly belong to them. She
could not help the way she felt and wondered if it were
wrong. Neither Lydia nor Clophelius had treated Moriah
with affection, so she never had felt close to them, but they
took her in as an infant when her life was in danger. She
owed them her regard.

As soon as Flavia left, Moriah summoned her courage and
broached the subject of the banquet to Clophelius where he
rested on a couch in the *bibliotheca,* a blanket over his withered legs. She was shocked to hear his answer.

"Of course you must go," he said brusquely, setting his
scroll on the marble tabletop. "Servius Antonus is an important man. He has numerous connections in the senate. And
those on the senate have the ear of Nero."

Stunned, Moriah looked at him, scarcely believing her ears.
"What of Mother? Surely you cannot expect me to attend a
banquet when she is in such ill health."

"Lydia shall not improve," he said, and the light seemed to
go out of his eyes with the words. His mouth narrowed. "You
are nearing three-and-twenty years of age, Moriah. It is well
past time I made you a match."

"Servius Antonus?" Moriah relived his bold stare raking
her at the games and felt she might be sick.

"Not necessarily. But it would not hurt for you to be seen. The guests at Antonus's feast are certain to be some of the most important people in Rome. . . ."

Moriah kept silent as he continued to explain the advantages of her attending such a banquet. For her to argue further would hinder her cause. She had been raised to be subservient and to accept the decisions made for her, whether she approved of them or not. How she wished that Paulus were here! He could talk to his uncle and urge him to change his mind. Usually Clophelius listened to Paulus.

Sudden memory of his failure to sway Clophelius concerning her attendance at the games caused Moriah to close her eyes in dismay. It was then that she knew her fate was certain.

❧

Paulus eased into the soothing warm water of the *tepidarium*. All around him, men and women reclined on couches, sat at the edge of the enormous pool, and waded through the waters of the public baths. He paid them little heed, grateful for this reprieve from his duties. Closing his eyes, he rested the back of his head against the cool ledge. Murmured talk and faraway laughter wafted over him, lulling him to rest.

Soon he became aware that someone crept behind him, trying hard not to be heard if the steady but soft clack of sandals coming closer was anything to go by. Whoever it was tried too hard to remain silent, in his opinion. Paulus stiffened, waiting. When the right moment came and he knew the intruder was directly behind, he quickly raised his arms and grasped the calves of the man. In one swift move, Paulus managed to throw his possible assailant into the water.

The man came up, spluttering and filling the air with foul language, eliciting curious stares in their direction. Seeing whom he'd attacked, Paulus threw back his head and roared with laughter.

"I see no humor in this," the man said brusquely, shaking the water out of his dark blond hair, much like a dog would. "As you see, I've not visited the changing room. And this was a new toga, I'll have you know." He took the few stairs out of the pool, the heavy, dripping folds of clothing clinging to his skin.

"Quantus, I beg pardon," Paulus told his childhood acquaintance, his mirth receding. "I had no idea it was you who so stealthily stalked me. You should not have underestimated me, my friend. After I've given almost half my life to the empire, the reflexes of a soldier are long ingrained in me."

"One of these days your glib tongue will be unable to protect you," Quantus muttered, squeezing the water from his toga. "It's a wonder those in charge of the baths have not thrown you out already."

Paulus laughed. "They do not dare!"

Despite his obvious desire to stay angry, Quantus grinned. "I suppose I should have known better than to sneak up on an officer of the guard. And I suppose I must pardon you, or the gods may become angry, and I might suffer a fate worse than this," he joked, lifting a fold to his wet clothing.

"Why have you sought me out, Quantus?" Paulus eased back against the wall. "I seem to remember your fondness is reserved for the theater and not the public baths."

"You speak in truth, but I have something of great importance to share, and this is where I was told you would be. First, I am for the changing room. If I must have a bath, at least allow me to take it in its proper form."

Paulus watched Flavia's brother walk away. It never ceased to amaze him that Quantus was related to that spiteful woman, though they did resemble one another in looks.

Within minutes, Quantus stepped into the *tepidarium* and took a place beside Paulus. He looked past him, an amused light in his eyes. "Perhaps my return was too hasty," he mused.

Paulus followed his friend's gaze to where a lovely woman sat on the other side of the pool in a short *tunica*. She stared at Paulus, a soft smile tilting the corners of her mouth.

Paulus looked away and back to his friend. "You said you had something you wished to share with me?"

Quantus's eyes widened when he noted Paulus's disinterest in the woman. "You have been away too long, my friend! Does the army allow you no pleasure? Have you forgotten how to partake of it? Venus beckons to you, and you turn away. Would that she might look at me in such a manner!"

Paulus shrugged, tired of pleasures that soon waned, their excitement never lasting. The wine, the feasting, the women—all left a bitter taste in his mouth come morning. Once his commission in the guard was over, Paulus entertained the idea of settling down. A pair of prized blue eyes as captivating as the sea came to mind. Only these eyes were set in a face surrounded by an abundance of raven black hair.

Quantus grew sober. "What I have to tell you is not good news. But I care for Moriah as a sister, as do you, and I do not wish ill fortune to come her way."

The mention of Moriah made Paulus tense. "What have you heard?"

At Paulus's loud query, Quantus looked at the few people within hearing distance. One man made no effort to conceal his interest but stared directly at them. "Perhaps we should move to the *caldarium,* where there is bound to be more privacy."

Paulus did not hesitate but followed Quantus out of the pool and wrapped a towel around his hips. He walked across the vast room and into another, this one filled with steam.

A slave secured a container of fragrant olive oil and a bronze strigil upon Paulus's request. Paulus covered his body with the oil, then proceeded to scrape it off with the curved end of the strigil. He turned to where he knew Quantus stood; the steam the boilers produced hid him. "Tell me," Paulus ordered tersely.

"Father mentioned that Servius Antonus has exhibited an unusual amount of interest in Moriah," Quantus replied.

"Yes," Paulus said curtly. "I became aware of that fact at the games."

"Flavia told me what happened. Poor Moriah," Quantus sympathized. "But do you know also, my friend, that a rumor is circulating among Nero's court concerning Moriah's parentage? It has been suggested that her true father was a well-known tribune who was later found to be a traitor to the empire and duly executed. Though you and I know the rumor is unfounded and Moriah has no connections with such a man, I fear she may be in danger. The tribune in question—a Rexus Caspus—was a powerful man and influential with the people. If Nero suspects the rumor is true and Caspus has an heir—even though she is only a woman—there is no telling what he might do, especially with Poppaea to whisper lies into his ear."

Paulus inhaled sharply. "Who would spread such a tale?"

"I know not, but I suspect the Prefect Tigellinus. He is always at the ready to make someone look bad in Nero's eyes. Perhaps there's no reason for concern, Paulus. I only thought you should know what I heard from Father."

Paulus soberly pondered Quantus's words.

"Likely, if the emperor wills it, Moriah will be brought before him and have a chance to assure Nero that she's not a Christian and a traitor to Rome, as this Rexus Caspus was," Quantus continued. "Once Nero looks upon her quiet beauty and her childlike innocence, surely he will be swayed in her favor."

"You forget Octavia. He killed her without an ounce of remorse." Paulus kept his voice low, aware that the very walls themselves could have ears. It was no secret that their great emperor was guilty of killing not only his wife, but also his mother at Poppaea's wish. Yet it was dangerous to talk in a bad light about Nero.

"Yes, it is so," Quantus amended. "But we are discussing an entirely different situation."

"I agree. Moriah is innocent and beautiful, as you have stated. Perhaps we should be concerned Nero may see this as well and take her for his own, to live as one of his concubines."

There was a chilling pause, though the air was hot and steamy. At last Quantus spoke. "Do not borrow trouble, my friend. Have you not heard? Father said Nero has complained of the stench filling Rome now that the days grow hotter and talks incessantly of returning to Antium. He shall leave soon, as I imagine you shall do also. I don't think you need fear that Nero will summon Moriah at this time."

Paulus grimaced. If Quantus were correct about Nero's decision to leave, which could mean that Paulus and his men would accompany their emperor if his cohort was chosen, who then would protect Moriah from Antonus—assuming Nero did not summon her to his palace beforehand?

"Perhaps this will all come to nothing," Quantus said. "Rumors have a way of dying when something of more interest comes to light."

Paulus threw down his strigil and stormed from the *caldarium* and into the *frigidarium*. Twice he swam the pool's length, allowing the icy cold water to cool his boiling blood.

So the secret was out, and Moriah's future was at stake. Quantus had never been told the truth. No one had except for Paulus and his family. And Paulus fervently hoped it remained so and that the rumors would quickly diminish. He could deal with a snake like Servius Antonus or anyone else who dared to get near Moriah. Yet when it came to their emperor, his hands were tied. If Nero were to summon Moriah to his court and gaze upon her beauty, Paulus was convinced he would never see her again.

ঌ

Sinista applied jasmine-scented oil to Moriah's damp back. Taking a strigil, the slave slowly began to scrape off the film.

Moriah was thankful she did not have to visit the public baths of Rome. Her father was one of the fortunate few who could afford such a private luxury in his house. Sinista helped Moriah dry off, then held a red tunic open, into which Moriah slid her arms. Nervous, she pulled the silk edges of the robe around her body and walked into her *cubiculum*. The hour had arrived.

She stood silent as Sinista and Sahara fussed over her. Sinista showed her a beautiful *stola* of shimmering twilight blue that twinkled with the lights of a thousand stars. Moriah gave a vague nod. She did not care what she wore. She wanted nothing to do with this banquet and counted the hours until it would be over and she would again be safe at the house.

The *stola* bore long filmy scarves of the same twilight blue clasped at each shoulder. They streamed down Moriah's back in a graceful fall to the hem of her skirt. A thin twisted cord of gold was wrapped around her waist, underneath the scarves. For the occasion, Sahara used tongs heated on the brazier to curl portions of Moriah's hair at the front and dressed it in a more elaborate style than Moriah was accustomed to wearing. Though she did not care for the intricate network of loops at the back, she offered no complaint. A linked necklace of gold encircled Moriah's neck. Matching earrings with pearls dangled from her ears. A ring of small gold beads with a pearl in its middle was slipped onto her forefinger.

When Flavia's litter arrived at the Dinoculus residence, Moriah was prepared, her manner stoic. Woodenly she approached the rectangular conveyance, which six Numidian slaves carried on long rods atop their shoulders. Carefully it was lowered so that she could step inside. The silk drape was pulled back revealing the pillowed confines within.

Her mind in turmoil over what lay ahead, Moriah paid little attention to the uneven ground, and the toe of her sandal caught in the crack between two flagstones. She pitched forward, hastily bringing her hands in front of her to break her fall—but she never hit the pavement.

Running steps struck the ground and strong hands swiftly grabbed her waist from behind, steadying her, then instantly dropped away. Once she regained her wits, Moriah turned to thank her rescuer. She gave a soft gasp when she saw Aidan. From where had he come so suddenly? Clophelius must have sent him to the city on an errand. He did that often since he himself never left the house.

Moriah experienced a strange breathlessness as she gazed up

at Aidan, though he didn't look at her. Standing as close to him as she did, she could feel his warmth, and it was both comforting and exhilarating. Heat tingled through her. Muttering a quick "thank you," Moriah turned and hurried into the litter, her face feeling as though it were ablaze.

Flavia reclined inside, looking lovely and bored in a rose-colored *stola* bound with gold cord. Her intricate necklace and earrings were of hammered gold as was the snake bracelet she wore on her upper arm. Gold dust powdered her hair. Obviously upset about something, the blond gave a cool nod to Moriah and remained silent.

As the litter was carried downhill, Moriah continued to survey Flavia's grim countenance. Was Flavia angry with her? Perhaps she still harbored feelings for Servius and did not appreciate his interest in Moriah. Well, Flavia could have him! That would be a great burden off Moriah's shoulders.

Once they reached Servius's house on the Aventine Hill, Moriah walked beside Flavia through the arched entrance, unable to quench the feeling that she was walking into her own private arena.

૨๑

Uneasiness clawed its way into his spirit as Aidan tended his master and bathed him. While he served him the light snack of *merenda,* the disquiet remained. Aidan's thoughts moved to his lady and their recent talk in the garden. How would Clophelius respond if he were to share with him what he had told Moriah? With censure or even wrath? Moreover, if Aidan admitted his Christianity, how did he know that Clophelius, who openly voiced his hatred of Christians, would not let the fact slip to Senator Valerius, who in turn might mention it to Nero? For himself, Aidan was not afraid. He had faced danger many times both as a child in his village and here in Rome. Yet he did not wish to put his brothers and sisters in Christ in possible jeopardy.

As Clophelius often did, he began to talk aloud, though he did not engage in conversation with Aidan or the two other slaves who stood in the room, awaiting orders. Rather, he liked the sound of his voice and enjoyed holding discussions with himself.

"Imagine Paulus becoming angry when he learned Moriah was to attend Servius's banquet this very night. He acts as if I do not desire what is best for the girl." Reaching toward a copper platter, Clophelius plucked up a cluster of plump red grapes and popped several into his mouth. Chewing his food, he continued. "Have I not provided well for her these many years? Have I not clothed her in fine linens and jewels and given her all the benefits of wealth—indeed, treated her as my own daughter?"

Alarmed, Aidan stopped pouring wine into Clophelius's goblet. Moriah in the company of Antonus? Aidan tensed, his grip on the handle of the pitcher tightening. He forced himself to resume pouring the red liquid into the golden chalice, which he then gave to Clophelius.

Now he understood the reason for his uneasiness. Perhaps he could slip away from the house before the meeting with Peter began, though he had no idea in what part of the city Servius Antonus resided.

Lord God, help her! Aidan's eyes slid shut as he silently— but fervently—began to pray.

❧

Servius signaled to an Armenian slave, who stood nearby with arms crossed over his bare chest. The heavyset man rapidly clapped his hands three times, and the melodic notes from the string cithara were silenced. A group of exotic Asian dancers wearing colorful gauze tunics hurried into the room next to the banquet table. An African man started to beat a drum slowly, and the women began a sensual dance. Cymbals rang on their fingertips, punctuating their every movement.

Moriah looked away, uneasy. From the moment the banquet had started, she'd experienced a strong desire to leave. Throughout the feast—which began hours ago and would continue until early morning, growing wilder as each hour passed if the present behavior of the guests was anything to go by—Servius's gaze rarely wavered from Moriah's form.

Fearful of what might happen to her or her family if she caused offense, she smiled at his foolish riddles and poems and, to his apparent delight, blushed at his lewd ones. Flavia's couch was at the end of the room, and Moriah was often aware of the blond's glances directed her way.

"Try some, Moriah," Servius coaxed, putting a fingerful of goose liver to her lips.

His intimate action unnerved her, and she jerked her head sideways, her hand almost knocking over her goblet. Nervous, she tried to inch away, as much as was possible on the long couch where she reclined next to him. Any farther and she would go over its bronze edge.

"No, thank you," she said quickly. "I prefer the hummingbird tongues." So saying, she reached for one from a platter a nearby slave set on the table and popped the crispy morsel into her mouth.

Servius grimaced at her deliberate evasiveness and put the brown paste to his own mouth. A slave came up behind them, offering yet another platter of food, and Servius reached for a serving of lamprey. Moriah chose some of the jellyfish with roe, though she was not certain she could eat it. If she busied herself with food, perhaps Servius would leave her alone. She hoped in vain.

As Moriah reached for another hummingbird tongue, Servius's hand shot out and his fingers clamped around her wrist. Alarmed, she looked his way. His eyes were bold, glazed from too many refills of wine. They roamed over her form, then returned to her face.

"Kiss me, Moriah," he rasped, and his other hand went to the back of her head, forcing her face close to his.

Immobilized from shock, Moriah did nothing to fight back as his wet lips covered hers. Obviously mistaking her lack of reaction for acceptance, he grasped her around the waist and tried to pull her to him. Terrified, Moriah pushed hard against his shoulders. Even her small effort was successful because Servius was drunk and off-balance.

His eyes were pained. "Why do you torture me so, daughter of Venus?" His hold painfully tightened on her wrist, and his words grew more fervent. "Food has little enjoyment for me this month past. Nor can I sleep since first I met you. I held this banquet tonight as a means of getting you here. What spell have you cast over me, my beauty? Why do you torment me so?"

She shook her head, wishing only for escape.

"Marry me," he breathed.

"I—I. . .my father—" Moriah stuttered, even more alarmed by his passionate proposal than she had been by the unwanted kiss. She would never marry such a man if she could help it! Yet she knew the danger of insulting one of Rome's prominent citizens.

"I will deal with your father," Servius said, his manner assured. "The house of Antonus is of great repute and wealth. He will consent to the match." His eyes seemed to glow. "Let us go somewhere more private, Moriah, that I may more fully gaze upon your beauty. Let us go to the garden and worship the god Eros, clasped in one another's arms underneath a canopy of stars." His hand moved to her waist and his fingers dug in deeply as he again tried to pull her close.

A woman's scream rent the air followed by a man's ribald laughter. Servius dropped his hand from Moriah in surprise. They both looked to another grouping of couches where a guest had grabbed one of the dancing girl's scarves, bound at her waist, and attempted to pull the woman to him. She resisted, trying to fight him off, while several guests laughed and offered shouts of encouragement to the man. The beat of the drums intensified, and the crowd grew more frenzied.

Some of the women began to dance wildly around the room, laughing and running from the men who chased them. Two male guests each pulled on a woman's arms, until one succeeded in pulling her away from his rival and kissed her.

Shouts, screams, and wild laughing filled the air as the banquet turned into a celebration to Bacchus, god of wine and revelry.

Disbelieving, Moriah watched Flavia jump onto the lap of the male guest next to her and lock with him in wild embrace. She knew this was what Flavia had spoken of in the past, what she had often encouraged Moriah to take part in, and her mouth filled with bile.

"No," she whispered, then more loudly, "No!"

Hoping their host might put an end to the madness, Moriah turned to him in appeal. An excited gleam lit his bloodshot eyes as he watched his drunken guests. His gaze turned her way, his expression heavy with desire.

Before he could grab her again, Moriah jumped from the couch and fled the room, ignoring Servius, who called for her to come back. The excited shouts of the guests rose above the rapid drumbeats and followed Moriah out to the *peristylium*. Terrified that Servius or one of his brawny guards might be in pursuit, Moriah hurried past shielding dark trees and shrubs, ignoring the pain as twigs and thorns scraped her arms and legs and tore at her *stola*.

Nearing the door at the entrance, she chanced a look over her shoulder. No one followed. She breathed a shaky sigh of relief, grateful to have escaped. As she let herself out into the black night, she was doubly thankful that Servius had been too drunk to give chase. She could hardly believe this was the city that called itself civilized!

Hurrying down the hill with no idea where she was going, Moriah knew only that she must get away.

☙

Aidan pulled the mantle closer about his face as he walked down the torch-lit road, keeping to the shadows. The meeting let out long ago, and he had learned from one of the followers of the Way the general vicinity of Servius's house. As Aidan traversed the dangerous thoroughfares, noisy with clambering carts and wagons laden with merchandise, he wondered if his feeble attempt was in vain. Even if he did locate the residence, he could not very well enter the building and wrest Moriah away from the man's clutches.

The thought of her in Servius's arms made him feel sick in his gut, and he increased his pace. Aidan had no idea what he would do, but he could not simply stand by and do nothing when he knew there was danger.

A woman's scream, coming from afar, trembled through the night.

Startled, Aidan came to an abrupt stop, then took off running up a short flight of stairs, through an archway, and down another street in the direction from which he thought the sound came. No one was there.

He tried to control his rapid breathing as he stood, listening beyond the rumble and creak of moving wheels, the warrior instincts of his former clan rising within him. Again, he heard a scream, but it cut off suddenly as though stifled.

Enraged that some helpless woman was in danger, Aidan raced down the street, brushing past several creeping wagons, and turned a corner and then another, hoping he was not too late.

He came upon two men in a narrow alley. The tall one stood behind a struggling woman whose dark hair had come unbound and streamed past her waist. The man's hand covered her mouth and his arm was wrapped tightly around her heaving chest. The smaller man tried to grab her flailing legs.

Moriah!

The barbaric blood of Aidan's ancestors boiled within his veins. A fierce anger such as he'd not felt since the night the Romans killed his entire family tore through him. Letting out a bloodcurdling howl of rage, he threw himself onto the man near Moriah's legs. Grabbing him in a bone-crushing hold, he lifted him high in the air and flung him against the wall as though he were weightless.

The man yelped in pain and scrambled awkwardly to his feet, intending to retaliate. Yet upon seeing his attacker was a tall, muscular barbarian, who at this moment was holding his partner in a fatal headlock, he panicked and fled down the street, nursing his wounded shoulder.

Aidan tightened his grip around the other man's neck, waiting to hear the satisfying crunch of bone, a base part of his nature yearning for it. Instead, he heard the quiet but commanding voice in his spirit. *Aidan—no!*

Recognizing to whom the voice belonged, Aidan groaned and forced himself to loosen his hold on the man. The attacker fell to the ground, coughing and wheezing, gasping for breath. When he could finally breathe, he threw a fearful look at Aidan and scurried backward, crablike, until he was some distance away. Then he jumped to his feet and fled down the alley.

Anger swiftly changed to concern for Moriah, and Aidan moved toward her. She drew back, eyes wide with fright. He felt as though a spear had been thrust through his heart. Swallowing hard, he noticed the dark bruise covering her swollen cheek and forced himself to approach more slowly. Fresh anger engulfed him at the men's rough treatment of her, but he outwardly remained calm.

"My lady?" His voice came out low and shaky with emotion.

෴

In confusion, Moriah stared at Aidan. What had happened to the gentle slave she knew? She did not know this man who stood before her. So how could she be certain his motives were no worse than Servius Antonus's or of those two vile men who had grabbed her and hurt her and forced her into this alley? When Aidan dealt with them, he reminded her of a gladiator in the arena. Even now she could see a wild, untamed look in his eyes—like a lion excited about the kill. Was everyone in Rome mad? First the banquet and now this. She shuddered and shrank closer to the building's wall.

"My lady," Aidan said again. Slowly he lifted his hand, then seemed to think better of it and dropped it to his side. "I apologize for frightening you. When I saw those men doing you harm—" He broke off and shook his head, his mouth narrowing as he briefly averted his gaze to the flagstones.

His emotion-ridden words helped to ease a good deal of her sudden inexplicable fear of him, and she saw that remorse and concern had replaced the bloodlust in his eyes. Still, she gave a slow nod, uncertain.

"Did they. . ." He hesitated as though it were difficult for him to go on. "Did they harm you?" His meaning was clear.

Moriah shook her head. Her legs trembled in the aftermath of what had almost befallen her. Her fingertips scraped the wall as she tried to clutch it to keep from falling, and what little strength she still possessed seemed to gush from her in one uncontrollable wave.

Aidan reached for her. This time she had no desire to draw back and was grateful when he scooped her up into his solid, strong arms.

"I have friends nearby," he said. "We will stop there and give you time to recover before I take you back to the house."

Moriah vaguely nodded. Her earlier fear of him vanished as the sudden realization came to her that he most certainly had saved her virtue—perhaps even her life. True, she had never seen him act with such unbridled rage, something she never would have believed Aidan capable of had she not witnessed it. Yet deep within she knew he would never hurt her. She could trust him.

Resting her head against his warm shoulder, Moriah derived comfort from the protective feel of his muscled arms and wearily closed her eyes.

six

Aidan hurried down the narrow streets with Moriah, repeatedly dodging carts and wagons. After a time, he came to a wooden arched door and gave three sharp raps, then he paused and gave two more—a signal informing those within that a friend stood on their doorstep.

A stout woman opened the door, her eyes widening when she saw Aidan with Moriah resting like a limp doll in his arms.

"Aidan! Come in—quickly," she said, pulling him inside and darting a glance around the dark street. Wheels rumbling over stones from somewhere nearby drew closer, and swiftly she closed the door. "I am Anna," she told Moriah. "You are welcome here for as long as you need to stay."

"What happened?"

Hearing the gruff voice from the far part of the room, Moriah turned her attention that way. A man with gray hair and a beard walked toward them across the earthen floor.

"Rufus!" Aidan exclaimed in surprise. "It is good to see you, my brother. Is Peter here as well?"

Moriah's heart gave a little jump. Peter? The apostle who had known her father?

"No, he had other business in the city," the man said. "I came alone."

Aidan gently deposited Moriah onto one of two rough, wooden benches near a table, and she curiously looked at the man who had joined them. His carriage was tall, husky, his hands quite large. In his youth, he must have possessed great strength and perhaps still did. Yet the look in his brown eyes was kind, putting her at ease.

"Is there trouble?" Rufus asked.

Grimly, Aidan related the account of the evening to the

small gathering. Anna comforted Moriah by offering her a dipper of water and handing her a cool, damp cloth to place on her still throbbing cheek. Grateful, Moriah held the compress to her face while studying the man across from her.

"Am I to understand that you are acquainted with the apostle Peter, who was with the man called Jesus—the man crucified for claiming to be the Son of God?" she asked, though it hurt to talk. Still, she had to know.

He looked at her solemnly and nodded. "I have known Peter many years."

Her heart skipped a beat, and her mouth went suddenly dry despite the water she had just sipped. "Please—where can I find him? He met my father in Jerusalem, and I must speak with him. There are questions I have."

"Your father is from the Holy City?"

"He was a tribune at the time of the man called Jesus. His name was Rexus Caspus, and my mother's name was Helena. I am told she was from Corinth."

Recognition sparkled in his eyes, and he smiled, enhancing the craggy lines in his face. "You are Moriah," he said as though just discovering something wonderful.

She blinked, startled. "You know me?"

"I saw you not long after you were born. I was a young man at the time and traveled with Peter even then in my hunger to hear the Word. He said a blessing over you, at your parents' request, and prayed for your continued protection. I also remember that a prophecy was spoken over you that day. . . ." His words trailed off, and he looked thoughtful. "Do you know what your name means, Moriah?"

Eyes wide, she shook her head.

"Mount Moriah is the mountain where God made a promise to His people through our father Abraham and later through our Lord Jesus, who was crucified in that same region. It was there that Abraham's faith was tested, and because he was obedient to God, he received the promise."

"The promise?"

"Yes. Through the promise, fulfilled through Jesus the *Christus,* those who partake of it become children of God and belong to Him as members of His family."

Belong! Of all the words Rufus spoke, none struck Moriah so strongly as that one word. Nervous, she cleared her throat. "Will you please tell me more about this promise your God made with His people?"

Rufus smiled and complied. When he spoke of the man called Jesus, whom Rufus had known for all three years of His ministry, the very air around them felt charged. An intense light burned in his eyes, as if a flame had been lit from within, much like the light she'd seen burning in Aidan's eyes on previous occasions. Strange tingles ran through Moriah as he spoke.

"I have listened to all you have told me," she said some time later, "though there is still much I do not understand. My father was responsible for Jesus' death on the cross. How could your God possibly forgive someone for killing His only Son?" Her words came out a little fearfully. She was certain there must be a hidden decree in their law, and neither her father nor she could belong to this family of God.

Rufus thought a moment. "Have you heard of a man by the name of Paul? Or perhaps you may know him by his former name, Saul. He is a Roman citizen, though he's a great leader of the Way and a good friend. Recently he was under house arrest, here in Rome, though he is in the city no longer. Upon his release, he left and continued his travels."

Moriah shook her head. "His name is not familiar to me."

"Saul is responsible for the deaths of hundreds of Christians— men, women, and children. He despised Christianity and did all in his power to stop it."

"I fail to understand. If he is against the Christian sect, then why—"

"Ah, but you did not let me finish, Child," Rufus inserted patiently. "Paul was once this man known as Saul of Tarsus. After a remarkable incident on the road to Damascus, he became fully aware that Jesus is the Christ, the Anointed One, and turned his life over to Him. The Lord forgave Paul for all past wrongdoings, and he now belongs to the family of God."

"If Peter were here, he would tell you that he also is proof of God's forgiving love," Anna put in. "After three years of friendship and trust, he betrayed the Master at a moment when He needed those closest to Him—by claiming he did not know Him. Not once, but three times. Yet Jesus forgave him, too."

Aidan swallowed hard and cleared his throat, feeling a powerful need to unburden himself. "Tonight—when those men harmed my lady, I—" He broke off and looked away, ashamed to continue.

"Yes, Aidan?" Rufus asked quietly, encouraging him. Aidan looked up into understanding eyes that held no condemnation. It was as though Rufus already knew what he was going to say.

"I wanted to kill them and almost did."

"But you chose not to."

"A voice within stopped me," Aidan agreed, his tone reflective. "A voice I have heard before."

Rufus smiled. "Ah, yes. The voice of the Holy Spirit living inside you. God understands your problem, Aidan, your war with the flesh. How well we all understand, though none of us is tempted in quite the same way. With some, it's the lust for women, some are drawn to wine, some covet money, and still others lust for blood."

Aidan nodded, his eyes downcast.

"Be comforted, my friend," Rufus continued. "He understands your weaknesses, not only because He made you and knows you, but also because He came down in the form of a Man who suffered and was tempted though He never sinned. And tonight, when your flesh yearned to do one thing, you were obedient to the voice of God. I should think our Lord is pleased with you."

At the man's encouraging words, the worry that had plagued Aidan vanished like the mist over the sea when the sun breaks through. He sagged in relief and smiled for the first time that night.

Anna's husband, Nereus, came from the back room, and they talked a few minutes longer until Aidan announced it was time to go. Sunrise was at hand, and he felt an urgency to return to the house. Rome's banquets often lasted throughout the night and on into early morning, and Moriah probably would not be expected back at this time, it was true; yet neither would it do for her to be seen in Aidan's company so late at night.

Moriah, too, must have realized the situation. She stood and thanked her host and hostess for their temporary haven of safety, then she faced Rufus and quietly thanked him for answering her questions.

Rufus laid a hand on her shoulder, his gaze riveting. "Consider this. God has a plan for you, Moriah. One of great magnitude. I knew this from the moment I saw you when you were but an infant. Seek Him, and you will find your answers."

Confusion and something akin to fear spread across Moriah's face. She gave only a slight nod, then turned and looked at Aidan. He regarded her briefly, amazed by Rufus's words.

Though Peter had recently said something similar to him, that God had an important calling for Aidan's life, Aidan wished he could partake of the plan God had for Moriah as well. To walk alongside his lady for the rest of his days, even as only her servant, both of them fulfilling a shared mission of the Lord's choosing, was a vision he'd begun to entertain not only in slumber but in his waking hours as well. Lately, especially after his late-night talk with her, Aidan had experienced a strong desire to preach the gospel as freely as Peter and Paul did. Yet his role as slave in a household that forbade talk of Christianity limited such opportunities.

"Shall we go, my lady?" he asked, masking the futile hope that had arisen.

She nodded, and together they moved outside into the murky gray world that acted as a harbinger of the dawn.

❧

Over the next few days, Moriah pondered her conversation

with Rufus. To say she understood all that was said would have been an untruth. Moreover, it alarmed her that the God of her parents expected some unknown thing from her. First, her maid had declared it, then Rufus did. Still, Moriah was determined to attend the next meeting. These Christians could not be so terrible if the character of Jesus' disciple was anything to go by. Then, too, there was Aidan.

Nearby, the sound of hobnailed sandals clattered across the mosaic tiles. Curious, Moriah hurried down the corridor toward the sound. She almost ran into Paulus, who had just exited the *bibliotheca*.

"Paulus! I did not know you were here."

The harsh planes of his face softened. "Moriah—you are well?"

"I could ask the same of you. You do not look as though you bring good tidings."

He grimaced, the fury jumping into his eyes again when his gaze landed on her cheek. "I heard about the banquet Uncle forced you to attend."

She looked away, her hand instinctively going to the light bruise she still bore from the horrible incident four nights earlier. His jaw clenched.

"I tried to arrive in time to help you, Moriah. But I was intercepted by one of my men with an order to meet with the prefect. I have been unable to get away until this afternoon."

Moriah nodded, still not looking at him. His firm grip went to her upper arms, forcing her gaze upward in surprise.

"Did Servius harm you? Did he put that bruise on your face? If he did, so help me, I'll kill him." The statement was even more chilling due to the low timbre of his words.

"No, Paulus. I left before he could do me harm."

"Then he did try to harm you?"

"I think he would have done so if I hadn't escaped."

A sharp expletive erupted from his mouth, making Moriah wince. He calmed, dropping his hands from her arms. "Forgive me, Moriah. I am not angry with you. Rather, I am

frustrated with circumstances beyond my power to control."
He turned away, unfastening the strap of his helmet and tearing it from his head.

"What's wrong?" she asked quietly, fear prodding at her soul.

After an uncomfortable moment, he faced her, his manner resigned. "It seems Nero has again tired of Rome and has decided to return to Antium. My century leaves at the end of the week."

"But you only just returned!"

"There is nothing to be done. My loyalties are to my emperor." He said the last sardonically through clenched teeth. "I hate to leave you at this time, what with Servius breathing down your neck at every turn. But I have no choice in the matter. I must go."

She placed her hand on his arm. "I understand. All will be well." She gave him a tremulous smile, though she felt anything but peace.

Paulus shook his head at her weak attempt to reassure. He covered her hand with his. "There is something of great import I wish to say, Moriah, something I want you to consider." He seemed suddenly nervous and released his hold on her.

"For as long as I can remember, I've felt a strong affection for you. When my term in the guard is over, I desire to take you as my wife."

Moriah's eyes widened in shock, but he held up his hand to stop her when she would have spoken.

"No. Do not reply at this time. I ask only that you think on the matter and give me your answer upon my return. If I were your husband, you would be protected always, as I have told Uncle." Without meeting her eyes, he kissed her forehead. He seemed uneasy, more so than Moriah had ever seen him. "Be careful, little dove—I do not speak those words lightly. Stay close to the house."

Dismayed, Moriah studied his departing form. She did not wish to hurt Paulus; neither did she wish to marry him. As dear as he was to her, she had no desire to be his wife. She had always regarded him as a brother, though she had been told he was her cousin. Yet he was not that, either. Her brow creased. Why must life be so complex?

"My lady!"

Moriah turned to face the servant who called, startled by the worry lacing her voice. "Yes, Sinista. What is it?"

"Your mother. She. . ." The Egyptian's thin arched brows drew together. "You must come quickly!"

Alarmed, Moriah hurried past the slave and toward the family rooms. Upon entering the bedchamber, she drew a quick breath. Lydia's face was a pasty gray, and her eyes burned fever bright. Clearly, her condition had worsened.

"Come closer, Child," she rasped. When Moriah approached the bedside, Lydia reached for Moriah's hand. "I have always cared for you—though I know I've not shown it well." She clutched Moriah's hand in a fierce grip. "Since the night Deborah first brought you to me, you were my own. My child—the child I could never conceive." She began coughing and put the cloth to her mouth. When it was pulled away, Moriah noted with alarm that clots of red spotted the material.

"You must not speak, Mother. You must rest so that you may get better." Moriah helplessly stood, uncertain what to do. In her feverish state, Lydia was oblivious to the words she spoke. Though Moriah was aware of the truth concerning her parentage, Lydia did not know Moriah had discovered the truth. Yet she spoke to Moriah as to one who knew.

Half-closed eyes surveyed Moriah, and a feeble smile touched the cracked lips. "You are so beautiful—much like Helena was. How strongly you favor her! You have her grace and manner, as well. If I could have done anything for her, I would have. She was my friend." Her eyes closed, and another coughing fit shook her frail body.

"Please rest," Moriah insisted. "You must not talk."

Once the spell ceased, Lydia lay back among the pillows. Her eyes focused on some point beyond Moriah. "I met

Helena when she sold me a length of cloth. There was something about her that drew me to her many times after that. She shared stories of her faith—similar to Deborah's. I feared the wrath of the gods and goddesses to listen too closely at the time, but now that I am soon to die—Moriah! What if they were true? I no longer know what is truth and what is a lie. The gods and goddesses I served gave me nothing in return, though I once thought them responsible for bringing you here. But what if Helena's words were true? What if her God *is* the only God?"

She began to cough again. Moriah was at once confused and concerned to see fear dim the watery eyes. She tried to think of something—anything—to say in response. Yet she had no idea what to say because she was as yet uncertain of the answers.

Aidan. He would know what to say.

She motioned for Sinista and gave the order for Aidan to be brought to the *cubiculum*. The slave stood and blinked, obviously puzzled by the strange request in bringing the master's personal slave into the mistress's bedchamber. Moriah repeated her order, more harshly this time, and Sinista hurried away to comply.

Aidan soon appeared, and Moriah felt a wave of relief. His gaze met hers briefly, then lowered. Moriah stood by the bedside and listened while he answered Lydia's pointed and fearful questions. Again, as there had been in the garden, an excited glow lit his features and his voice as he spoke. He explained that the only way that leads to salvation for all mankind is through a personal acceptance of God's Son, Jesus the Christ. Moriah watched in amazement as a look of calm settled over Lydia's face.

"Thank you, Aidan. I believe I finally understand," Lydia said, her voice strained. "You may go."

He bowed. "My lady."

Moriah stared at Lydia's wan face, watching her eyes close in slumber, then she hurried from the room after him.

"Aidan?"

He turned and looked directly at her, his expression soft. Moriah felt as though the breath had been jarred from her body. A slave walked past bearing a large earthenware container, and Aidan quickly averted his gaze to a point beyond Moriah's left shoulder.

"I want to thank you for what you did," Moriah whispered, once the servant disappeared through a curtained portal. "I know it's dangerous for you to speak of your faith. Yet your words seem to have settled her. For that I am grateful."

"I am sorry I gave you the wrong impression, my lady."

Moriah blinked and looked up into Aidan's solemn countenance. "What do you mean?"

"Before Jesus left this earth, He made it clear it was everyone's duty to spread the gospel to any and all who would listen. He warned that there would be persecutions because of His teachings, but such things are not to stop us. My lady, the night we spoke in the arbor, I was wrong to temporarily withhold the Truth from you when I should have given you the answers to your questions the moment you asked them."

"You were concerned for your friends, as well as for your position in this household," Moriah said, completely baffled by his confession. "I understood that."

"Yet I spoke to you in a manner unworthy of a slave to his mistress. Well I know had I been in any other household in Rome, punishment would have been exacted for my insolence."

"Oh, Aidan," Moriah murmured before she could stop herself, "I no longer think of you as a slave. To me, you are so much more than that—" She broke off, her face going hot when she realized what she had said.

Dark blue eyes full of surprise searched hers, and time seemed to suspend itself. She licked her lower lip, then nervously caught it between her teeth.

The action brought his gaze to her mouth. He took a hasty, almost awkward, step back, his eyes again focusing beyond her left shoulder. "I am happy I please you, my lady," he said, his voice husky. "I must return to your father."

Moriah watched him move away until she could no longer see him. Her words had come unbidden to her lips, but once she uttered them, she realized how true they were.

The confusion that plagued her mind escalated. For where in this empire, with its many regulations, could there be a future for a patrician's daughter and a slave from Britain?

❧

Lydia lingered three days, then slipped away in her slumber. Gravely, Moriah studied the wasted form and marveled at the look of peacefulness on the still face. The wrinkles had almost completely disappeared, and Moriah was amazed at how youthful Lydia looked in death.

Had she responded to the message of salvation Aidan had shared with her? Moriah would never know, though Lydia had seemed to come to terms with dying, no longer fearing it. She had grasped Moriah's arm the previous evening, her eyes intense. "Aidan is a good man. He may be only a slave, but he speaks words of wisdom. Listen to him." After delivering that statement, she fell against the pillows, exhausted. Those had been the last words she spoke.

Moriah motioned for two servants to wash and prepare the body. Days from now there would be a procession to the *monumentum* to place the wrapped body in the family vault. Yet Moriah was too weary to think on the future, having stayed by Lydia's bedside almost continually, and she moved slowly to her room.

Stretching out on her stomach upon her bed, Moriah allowed a few quiet tears to roll down her cheeks. She was glad Lydia seemed to find peace at the end yet saddened to lose her. Though they never were close—all the more strange considering Lydia's words of gratitude about the day Moriah was brought to her as an infant—and Deborah spent more time with Moriah than Lydia ever had, Lydia would be missed.

Moriah's thoughts trailed to Aidan as they often did. She considered the words he had shared with Lydia. There had been such persuasion, such power in the message he spoke. Yet such teachings went against everything Roman. Still, what if there were truth to Aidan's words? What if his God was genuine?

Too exhausted to ponder the question more deeply, Moriah curled up on her pillows and closed her eyes.

&

Aidan hurried inside Clophelius's *cubiculum*. "You sent for me, Master?"

Clophelius lifted his head from silk pillows and propped himself up at Aidan's low words. His red-rimmed eyes were evidence of the pain he must be feeling since his wife's death, or perhaps an overindulgence of wine, or both. He motioned to his bodyguard to leave, then glanced at Aidan. Aidan stared past him, at the wall.

"Come closer."

Aidan obeyed.

"Closer still," Clophelius ordered, looking past Aidan, to the curtain covering the doorway.

Aidan moved to the edge of his master's couch, wondering at the man's clandestine behavior.

"Shortly before Lydia died, she made me vow to care for Moriah," Clophelius said, his voice low. "And it has recently come to my attention that her life might be in danger."

Aidan inhaled sharply. "Danger, my lord?"

"Shh! Hold your tongue." Clophelius briefly looked past Aidan. "A rumor about her has reached Nero, and I fear it is no longer safe for her in Rome. Until I can make arrangements to send her elsewhere, I want you to act as her bodyguard if and when she leaves the house. If I were to keep her within its confines, as I did when she was younger, such an action might feed the suspicions of those who could do her harm. Neither do I wish to alarm her with this news. Now that Nero is in Antium, likely she is safe. However, I want you to take no chances. Stay close by her side. Watch all who come near."

His mind a whirl of thoughts, Aidan could only nod.

Clophelius regarded him fondly. "You are a good slave, Aidan, and the only one of my household I truly trust. I cared deeply for my wife and intend to keep the vow I made her. Although it pains me to have you leave my company for even a short time, I am confident that you will watch over Moriah and see that no harm comes her way."

"As you wish, my lord," Aidan said with a small bow. Memory of the night he rescued Moriah almost two weeks ago came to the forefront of his mind. Had those men been sent by Nero to kidnap her and take her to him? Or had they acted for their own vile purposes?

Aidan grimaced. He would gladly give his life for Moriah. Already she claimed a piece of his heart—and that was almost as troubling as news of the possible danger that confronted her. How would he be able to deny his burgeoning feelings for his lady while spending so much time in her company? To dismiss his love for her and to pretend he did not care?

Swallowing hard, Aidan closed his eyes at the monumental task before him.

seven

"My lady, do you not think it time to return home?" Aidan asked quietly from behind Moriah as she perused a velvet-lined tray of shimmering jewels a pleased hawker pushed her way.

"For one as beauteous as you, I make very sweet deal," the practically toothless man told her with a smile.

"Your merchandise is quite lovely." Moriah picked up a ruby ring in an elaborate gold setting. "This would be perfect for Deborah. She has been so helpful to me these past weeks, and I wish to reward her kindness."

"My lady?"

At the impatience in Aidan's voice, Moriah turned in surprise. He struggled not to look at her. "We should return to the house. The hour is late."

"Very well, Aidan." She sighed and paid the amount the hawker requested, not bothering to barter. Again she turned Aidan's way. "I am ready."

Words deserted him. Rays of sunlight shimmered off her silky hair, teasing silvery blue highlights from the black strands. Most of it was styled in clusters of curls, gathered and hanging down the back of her *stola*—which exactly matched the color of her troubled blue eyes. A tight band squeezed around Aidan's heart, making it difficult for him to draw breath.

He gave a terse nod and walked back the way they had come, all the while strongly aware of her by his side. The fragrance of jasmine—her scent—lingered in the air, practically driving him mad. Last week he had told himself he could do this, the memory of their companionable talks in the garden fueling his certainty. He had come to look forward to the pleasurable discussions they would have without the need to

96

meet secretly, as well as to the time and opportunity given them. And it had been pleasurable. Too much so.

After a prolonged time in Moriah's company, Aidan had grown strongly aware of how her hair gleamed almost iridescent in strong sunlight. How her eyes crinkled at the corners when she laughed, and how white her teeth shone. How appealing and soft her lips appeared, like velvety petals from a rose. Furthermore, he carried these memories into the evening when she was no longer by his side and often into his dreams as well.

To allow improper thoughts of an emotion such as love to take their course would be folly on his part, he knew. He was nothing more than a slave—a piece of property belonging to the Dinoculus household. And she was the daughter of his master.

"Aidan—wait!" Moriah called to his back. "Is there truly cause for such haste?"

He didn't answer but forged ahead.

Drawing her brows together, Moriah hurried to catch up. Why did Aidan act so strangely? Was he repulsed by her company?

She had told Clophelius little of the assault, explaining only that a man rescued her and she escaped with the bruise on her face. She had been pleased he cared enough to assign her a bodyguard. She had been doubly pleased to learn it was Aidan.

Since that day, Moriah found any and every excuse to leave the house, secretly desiring time alone with Aidan, though she knew she should be ashamed of her obvious and devious actions. Certainly Aidan must know that she didn't make a habit of visiting the marketplace four times in a week. Is that why he was so testy this morning? Was he weary of spending time with her?

Not paying attention to her surroundings, she ran into the path of a litter being hurried across the road by slaves. She whirled in surprise, seeing that the slaves had also come to an abrupt halt to avoid running her over. In their confusion, they almost dropped the litter. A woman poked her head from inside the filmy curtain and gave her servants a harsh rebuke. Seeing Moriah nearby, she turned the force of her fury upon her and shouted obscenities.

Moriah's face went hot from a mixture of embarrassment and anger. Suddenly she felt the warmth of Aidan's reassuring presence behind, and it bolstered her courage. Moriah lifted her chin, quietly made her apologies, and strode away, leaving the irate woman ranting midsentence.

"Many pardons, my lady," Aidan said once they moved along the road a short distance. They entered a slave pavilion. "I should not have walked so quickly."

Moriah gave him a sideways glance and might have spoken, but a slave trader seemed bent on getting their attention, motioning to them and trying to interest them in a pair of blond Lygian twins. The women, who looked younger than Moriah, stood on a platform, their expressions anxious. The slave trader beamed at what he assumed to be Moriah's interest.

"They were the property of a deposed prince and would make excellent personal servants or entertainers," the man said. "And at a bargain price of only six hundred *sesterces* for the pair. Smile, you fools," he tersely ordered the women under his breath.

Moriah frowned at the trader. She moved away, and the man muttered something else, then approached the next possible conquest.

Moriah felt pity for the women and would have helped if she could. Yet she did not have Clophelius's permission to obtain servants for his household; that was Hermes's task. Nor did she have much money with her after buying Deborah's ring. Deborah. . .she had also been brought to Rome and sold as a slave. What would have happened to her dear friend if Moriah's mother had not purchased Deborah? Would she have been sold to a mistress or master as benevolent as Helena? Moriah doubted it.

Halting, Moriah looked over her shoulder. She sensed Aidan stop beside her in surprise. The two women were being led away by a thickset man who had just bought them. Moriah felt her heart drop.

"My lady," Aidan said quietly, breaking into her thoughts. "Do not be anxious for them. Come away and do not think of it." He gently took her elbow to steer her past a wine stall and the people milling around the area.

All of a sudden, a band of loud merrymakers drunkenly wove past, knocking into others. Aidan hurriedly pulled Moriah out of harm's way. Her back was pressed against his muscled chest, his arm loosely but protectively wrapped around her to prevent her from being trampled. Being held against him, as she was, produced more of an impact to her senses than the drunkards could have managed by knocking her down. Surely Aidan could feel the rapid pounding of her heart beneath his arm, matching the swift beats of his own heart that she felt against her shoulder blades. She swallowed hard and closed her eyes, resisting the urge to lay her head back against his collarbone.

Soon the way was clear again.

Yet Aidan did not release his hold.

Her breath caught in her throat at what this might mean, and Moriah slowly twisted around to face him. "Aidan?" she whispered, her hand tentatively moving to touch his shoulder.

The noisy crowd was forgotten as she stared up into intent blue eyes focused only upon her. His arm tightened around her waist, bringing her closer still. His expression was almost pained as his gaze roved her face and came to rest on her parted mouth. At last, his head began to lower to hers.

"Make way! Make way!" a tradesman cried atop a braying donkey that ran directly toward them.

Aidan hastily straightened and again pulled Moriah out of harm's path. After the danger was passed, he dropped his hold from around her waist and moved a short distance from her, leaving her feeling bereft.

"We must go," he said, his voice sounding odd. *"Cena* will be served soon."

Moriah nodded but had no idea what he'd just said. She was still reliving the kiss that almost was.

ह

"Mistress? Are you well? You have acted strangely since your return from the market. Can you not sleep?"

"I have no idea what ails me." Moriah looked away from the dark city and moved from the terrace toward her curious maid. "I find I am unable to rest."

"It is common to have trouble sleeping after losing a loved one. If you desire, I can rub scented oil into your temples—"

"Not tonight, Deborah," Moriah interrupted with an impatient wave of her hand. Realizing her words were unnecessarily curt, she softened her tone. "Go to bed. I will do so shortly."

"Yes, my lady. Again, many thanks for the lovely ring."

Moriah allowed a smile. "You deserve it, and so much more. You have been faithful, Deborah."

"It is always a pleasure to serve you."

Once Deborah left, Moriah looked out over the city again. Except for the occasional passersby, the night was still. Would that the stillness could seep into her troubled soul! Perhaps a visit to the garden might soothe her.

Barefoot, Moriah walked outside. The warm breeze caressed her face, and she inhaled the scent of freshly raked soil mixed with the sweet blend of flowers. Suddenly she noticed a cloaked figure standing in the shadows near the door in the wall.

"Aidan?" she murmured. Her heartbeats quickened, partly from fear, partly from hope.

The tall form hesitated, then stepped into the moonlight. She could see little of the person's features, since they remained hidden by the mantle covering his head.

"My lady," he said at last.

Relief and pleasure swept through her to discover it was Aidan. "Where do you venture this time of night?" She moved his way. "Is there another meeting?"

Again he paused before answering. "Yes."

"Why did you not tell me?" Moriah softly insisted. "I thought I made it clear that I wished to go with you when last we spoke of it."

"I did not think it wise, my lady."

"Did not think it wise? Whatever do you mean?" Moriah was confused by his strange words. "You have nothing to fear. I will not divulge your secret or endanger your friends—surely you must know that by now. Stay here. I will be only a moment."

Quickly she lifted the hem of her *stola* so that she could silently race to her bedchamber. Worried that Aidan would not be in the garden when she returned, Moriah grabbed her sandals and her darkest *palla* and fled the room. When she reached the arbor, relief swept through her to see him waiting.

No bench stood nearby, so she sank to the path to put on her sandals, not wanting to waste precious time to seek out a more appropriate place. Glancing up from the task of tying the last lace around her ankle, she caught Aidan watching her. His face was barely discernable in the faint glow of the moon, but he seemed disturbed.

"I did not wish to wake the household with the noise they make," she explained, motioning to her footwear.

"I know." He continued to stare at her exposed calf, then turned toward the arched door in the wall. "We must make haste," he said, his words clipped. "Stay close and keep silent. The city is dangerous at night, as you have discovered."

At Aidan's grim reminder, Moriah's heart beat fast, seeming to pulse in her ears, and she followed Aidan onto the dark street. She did not mind his giving the orders. In fact, she was grateful for it. Fear robbed her clarity of mind and speech. Was she acting in haste? Was this truly the proper course of action to take?

The walk seemed endless, and Moriah wished she had worn her sturdier leather shoes instead of her flimsy sandals. The click of her footwear sounded unusually loud on the stone path.

They darted beyond the city gates, under cover of several carts rumbling into the city, and toward low hills filled with sandpits. Moriah spotted bobbing yellow lights in the distance—evidently torches carried by others making their way to the catacombs. The people holding them appeared as dark, shapeless forms. Moriah trembled and focused on the way before her.

Aidan carried no torch, and Moriah was surprised he could see to traverse the road in the moon's glow when the white orb did decide to peek from behind the mass of gray clouds it wore for cover. Several times Moriah felt Aidan reach out to steady her from stumbling over rocks as she walked alongside him. As soon as she found her balance, he removed his hold from her arm and distanced himself from her.

Why? Was his cool behavior due to that moment in the marketplace when he almost kissed her? If the need for silence were not pressing, Moriah would have asked and made certain he knew she was not averse to such a show of affection from him—in fact, she eagerly welcomed it. But now was not the time for words. With every scrape of stones skittering across the path, Moriah's breath caught. Afraid to look over her shoulder, she wondered if enemies of the Christians had discovered the location of the clandestine meeting and were even now moving to harass or apprehend them.

Aidan must have sensed her uneasiness, for he lagged a step behind to whisper, "Do not fear, my lady. We are almost there."

The pleasing scent of tangy herbs laced his warm breath and caressed her cheek. Her mouth went dry, and she only managed a small nod in return. When he moved ahead, she drew her mantle closer about her throat with shaky hands.

Soon they approached a ditch. Aidan, obviously sensing Moriah's apprehension, put a hand to her elbow as they walked to the end where a closed gate stood. He picked up a stick and, in the lone light from the torch the huge gatekeeper held, scratched onto the dirt a line drawing of two sideways arcs intersecting at one end, resembling a fish.

"Peace be unto you, my brother," the burly man said, before allowing them entrance.

Moriah followed Aidan to a walled, roofless chamber with monuments strewn about. He tried to find a place closer to the entrance of the crypt, which led downward to the catacombs, but the way was thick with people. Numerous cloaked figures with hoods obscuring their features stood facing the crypt, waiting.

"Aidan," Moriah began uncertainly, fear beginning to take a stranglehold. Her breath was almost nonexistent in her tight throat. Whatever had possessed her to come to this place of death?

An elderly man stepped into the torchlight, and the quiet conversation ceased.

"That is the apostle Peter," Aidan whispered.

Moriah curiously studied the man who'd had such an impact on her father. He was tall, with long white hair, mustache, and a beard. A staff was in his hand. Now that she had talked to Peter's friend Rufus, Moriah no longer had the burning desire to question Peter, though she would still like to meet him.

Several people began to sing. Others joined in until the entire congregation sang praises to their God.

Lifting her gaze to the star-flecked sky, Moriah wondered. Did this Most High God and His Son Jesus, the *Christus,* hear the people who had gathered to worship Him? Or was He just another of the worthless and meaningless gods filling the temples of Rome?

She studied the uplifted faces discernable in the yellow glow of flickering torches. Even in such poor light Moriah could see that all these faces—some young, some old, some haggard, some strong—shared one trait: All seemed to be filled with joy and peace. How perplexing. These people were plebeians, though she spotted one or two fine cloaks denoting wealthy citizens among the group. What would these poor souls have to be joyful about?

The answer came swiftly, startling her. They belonged as one family, all worshiping the God they served.

A yearning, so intense it was painful, surged through her. She wanted what they had. She, with all her wealth and finery and personal slaves, was envious of these people—many of whose dark cloaks were frayed and torn and who bore faces thin from hunger.

When the apostle Peter began to speak, Moriah listened— truly listened—as he spoke of the Messiah who died so that all could come to know Him and live in His kingdom forever.

After the service ended, Moriah followed Aidan while he greeted the others. She recognized Anna and her husband, Nereus, and exchanged a quiet salutation with them. Aidan, his grip firm on Moriah's upper arm, then worked his way through the crowd to the front and introduced her to Peter. Rufus stood near and smiled at Moriah, and she smiled in return. She then looked at Peter. What struck her immediately was the glow coming from the apostle's dark eyes. He, too, seemed to possess a flame burning within.

Peter seemed as pleased to meet Moriah as Rufus had been and spoke several kind words about her father. He answered her questions about both her parents, though he didn't tell her anything she hadn't already learned. Still, Moriah was grateful for the opportunity to meet one of the important leaders of the Christians.

A man stepped up and urgently reminded Peter that it was time they departed. The apostle said a fond farewell to Moriah and Aidan, which they both returned, and Aidan led Moriah from the cemetery. As they walked toward the gate, several men clasped arms with him in greeting. To those men and women who spoke to her, Moriah smiled or nodded politely, saying nothing, absorbing everything. Her uncertainty concerning these Christians had been laid to rest. There was nothing dangerous about them; they performed no vile rituals as she had been told.

On the journey back, Moriah was quiet but not anxious as

she had been earlier. In fact, being alone with Aidan made her feel a little reckless and want more time in his company. Not long after they entered the city, Moriah recognized where they were and grabbed hold of Aidan's sleeve to gain his attention. Although it was late, she wanted to prolong the evening; she wanted more time with Aidan.

"I am weary," she said. "The way has been long. Let us rest before we continue to the house. I know of a place nearby."

When she led the way to the gardens Paulus had taken her to after the games, Aidan hesitated, as though he would protest. Through the trees, the palace loomed in the background.

"It is all right," Moriah insisted. "See? There is no one nearby. Nero is in Antium, and we are alone. Besides, Paulus told me that no one visits these gardens at night. We shall be safe."

Aidan still seemed uncertain, though he accompanied her up the hill and past the tall stately trees bordering the gardens. At Moriah's urging, they left the main path to walk down a narrow one—not much of a path at all and different from the one she and Paulus had taken. Aidan moved brushy overgrowth aside for Moriah until they came to a clearing with a small pond thickly surrounded by tall myrtles and cypresses.

"Oh, let us rest here," Moriah breathed. "Behold, the moon shining upon the black water. . . ." She inhaled deeply, glad to see that the bright moon had at last broken free of the thick clouds behind which it had hidden most of the night. "And the air is fragrant with jasmine. Do you like the scent of jasmine, Aidan?" She turned toward him.

He muttered something incoherent while reaching for the hood of his mantle to pull it away. A thin streak of black appeared on his hand. Without thought, Moriah grabbed his wrist and pulled it close.

"You've cut yourself!"

He jerked his hand from her grasp. "It is nothing. I scratched it among the thorns."

Moriah frowned. "Why is it that you act so strangely toward

me, Aidan?" She voiced the question that had tormented her for days.

"My apologies. I was unaware I acted in any such manner."

"You have become so distant of late."

"And what other way should a slave act toward his mistress?" he asked thickly, looking askance.

Boldly, heart pounding, Moriah stepped closer and cupped his cheek with her palm. His startled gaze swung to her steady one. "But I have told you, Aidan," she whispered. "I do not think of you as a slave."

Tense seconds passed. Without warning, his arm shot up and he grabbed her wrist, his countenance almost angry. Moriah gasped in surprise.

"And what do you offer, my lady? The same pleasures with which your friend Flavia entices men? The forbidden fruits—which are a trademark of Rome and its people—and go against the Christian teachings by which I abide?"

Forcefully, he pulled her hand from his jaw. "I want no such thing from you!" A tortured look filled his eyes. "And yet what I desire I can never have."

The pain Moriah felt at his rejection evaporated upon hearing his stilted words. "What do you mean?" she breathed.

He dropped his hold on her wrist. "Forgive me. I should not have spoken so. I forgot myself. It is late. We must return to the house before our absence is discovered."

"Aidan?"

Ignoring her, he pivoted on his heel and hastened away, exiting the bushes with a loud rustle. Moriah had no choice but to follow, her emotions a strange mixture of discouragement and expectancy. What had he meant by those puzzling words?

They returned to the main path, each one silent. A short time later, the unmistakable sound of hobnailed sandals clattered over stones, coming in their direction.

Startled, Aidan halted near a cypress, putting out his hand to stop Moriah when she would have walked farther. Quickly, he scanned the area. To the sides of them loomed nothing but more cypresses spaced far apart and beyond that a huge grassy area with the moon's bright glow encompassing the ground. The tree trunks were too narrow to hide behind. If he chose to take hold of Moriah's arm and retrace their steps to the pond and shielding overgrowth far behind them, the soldiers would surely hear or see.

Even as Aidan watched, their helmeted forms came closer, becoming distinguishable. If he could see them, they could surely see him and his lady. There was no escape. If they were caught here at this time of night, this close to the palace, it could mean death.

"Oh, Aidan, I'm so sorry," Moriah whispered, fear lacing her words. She put a hand to his cloak. "What shall we do?"

Making a split-second decision, Aidan turned to her, his mouth going dry when he considered what he was about to do. It was a feeble plan at best, but he could think of nothing else. With trembling hands, he pushed the hood of her cloak away from her face, hoping she would understand and not condemn him in light of the words he'd so recently spoken.

"Forgive me, my lady," he implored, his voice husky.

Moriah blinked. "For what?"

"For this," he whispered before lowering his mouth to hers.

Moriah clung to his solid shoulders, her limbs going weak. When Aidan pressed his hands to the middle of her back and lowered her to the earth, she went, unresisting. The feel of his muscled body and the heat of his mouth on hers caused her world to spin, and she barely heard the soldiers approach.

eight

"What goes on here?" a harsh voice demanded. "Stand to your feet!" The night air rang with the sound of a sword being drawn from its scabbard.

Aidan broke the kiss but continued to hold Moriah protectively in his arms.

"Stand to your feet, I say! Or would you prefer to taste the bite of my blade?"

Aidan rose from the ground, helping a shaky Moriah up with him. She quickly replaced the cloak over her head and pulled it close. Aidan stepped in front of her, blocking the men's view of her features, and faced their adversaries.

He had hoped when the soldiers came upon them, they would mistake Aidan and Moriah for a pair of young lovers enjoying a secret, late-night tryst and leave them be. But as he stared at the point of the sword now raised to his face, Aidan was certain his desperate plan had failed.

Please, God! Let them do what they want with me. But do not let them harm Moriah.

"Ah, leave him be, Cereus," a more jovial voice said from behind the man with the weapon. "He is obviously not a spy or a dangerous criminal to the empire. Can you not see? He is only having sport. Would that I could do the same instead of being assigned this accursed night duty!"

"Why are you here?" Cereus ignored his companion and addressed Aidan, who remained still. "Can you not speak?" the soldier insisted, his eyes narrowing. "Have you no tongue in your head?" The flat of the blade pressed against Aidan's jaw.

Deep within, Aidan felt the Spirit of the Lord instruct him to stay silent. He remained motionless, his steady gaze never leaving the soldier's face.

"It is probable that you have guessed correctly, Cereus. He must be dumb. No one would be fool enough to defy a Roman soldier with death so close at hand unless he was unable to speak."

"I fear you've become too lenient, Flebius. Yet this time I'm apt to agree with you." Cereus pressed the blade harder against Aidan's skin until the sword's tip barely broke the surface. "Is this true? Are you without speech?"

Aidan said nothing.

Cereus continued to stare at him, then slowly lowered his sword. "Very well. Take your sport elsewhere. Do not let me catch you near the palace again. Or next time it will be to the arena for both you and your woman. Go!"

Aidan turned and grasped Moriah's elbow. She drew her cloak closer over her face, escaping the soldiers' suddenly interested stares. Aidan held fast to her arm as they hurried away, the soldiers' vulgar comments and coarse laughter following.

When they had put enough distance between them and the soldiers and Aidan felt reassured the danger had passed, he pulled Moriah into the shadows of one of many temples lining the street so she could catch her breath. He wiped away the trickle of blood on his cheek.

"Are you all right?" Anxiously, he studied her, wishing he could see her features, but the hood of her cloak shielded them. "My lady?"

Moriah lifted her face to the moon's glow, turning huge eyes still glazed with desire and confusion his way. "You kissed me," she said softly, as if she could not believe he had done such a thing.

An uncomfortable lump rose to Aidan's throat. "Forgive me, my lady. I could see no other choice at the time. The soldiers did not jest when they spoke of the arena. I'm sorry that I was so bold—"

Lifting her hand, she placed her fingertips against his lips to still his words, then raised her eyes to his.

"I'm not," she whispered.

Aidan knew he should protest, but he had misplaced the words in a corner of his mind that suddenly was shut off to him. His heart thundered hard against his ribs, echoing in his ears. Her soft touch on his mouth and the memory of the feel of her in his arms clouded rational thought. Feelings concerning her that had been held in check for years rose to the surface to engulf him, and he gave up the inward battle, surrendering to the plea in her beautiful eyes, unwilling to fight any longer.

His hands moved to span her waist, and he drew her close, crowding out all the reasons why he should not do so. "Moriah," he said hoarsely into her silken hair, speaking her name for the first time.

Her exuberant response was practically his undoing. She wrapped her arms around his neck and eagerly offered her lips to him. Groaning softly, Aidan tightened his arms around her slender form and returned the kiss.

He wanted her—God help him—with every fiber of his being, he wanted her. Heart. Mind. Soul. Body. Every part of him ached for her. . .had always yearned for her to become his. . .and here she was in his arms.

Aidan broke the kiss, his breathing ragged. Quickly he stumbled back and turned, putting distance between them.

"Aidan?" she said from behind, her voice a mere thread.

Unable to speak, he briskly shook his head while trying to bring his turbulent emotions under control. He had come so close to falling into temptation. He would not let it happen again.

When his composure returned, he faced her. "My apologies. The fault was entirely my own."

"Fault?" Moriah shook her head. "I am an innocent in the ways between a man and woman, it is true, but what we shared. . .I see no blame to be placed, Aidan."

Warily he watched her slow approach yet remained as still as one of the temple statues inside the shadowed niches.

Moriah stopped in front of him. Hoping he would not

retreat, she lifted her hand to a lock of his mussed hair, unable to resist the temptation to gently push it from his eyes and over his shoulder. His head gave a slight jerk, but he did not move away.

"Consider this," she said, voice trembling. "I know only that I love you. I have for some time. And I believe you love me. I know you are not one to take your pleasure with any woman, as many of the men in Rome do. You do not give your kisses freely—"

"I did so tonight because of the soldiers," Aidan interrupted, his words brusque.

"I see no soldiers here."

He briefly closed his eyes. "My lady, the God whom I serve would not be pleased if I were to go against His teachings."

She shook her head in confusion. "Is your God against pleasure between a man and a woman who care for one another? Who *love* one another?" she asked softly, stressing the word.

Aidan swallowed hard. "No, my lady. But He has issued rules we must follow. Rules to protect His children. The pleasure of which you speak should only be shared between a man and his wife. Love—true love—is much deeper, much more wonderful than merely the physical. It involves everything, including a commitment. And it must have God at its core."

"I don't understand." Moriah shook her head, creasing her brow. "I've never heard such things. They are foreign to the way I've been taught. But surely—if what you say is true—is it not possible for us to share such a commitment, Aidan?" Her gaze held his, refusing to let go. "My feelings for you exceed merely the physical. Can you honestly tell me you don't feel the same about me?"

His head jerked back as if she had slapped him. "My lady, I am a slave! And you are the daughter of a patrician."

"The adopted daughter," she corrected. "My father was a tribune, but he was also a Christian. As are you."

"It makes little difference. Can you see Clophelius agreeing to such a match? It is inconceivable!"

"I care not! I care only for you." Desperately Moriah clutched the folds of his cloak with both hands and laid her head against his chest and his swiftly beating heart. "Tell me you care, Aidan. Tell me you love me as I love you," she whispered. She lifted her face to his, silently beseeching him. "Show me. . .as you did before. . . ."

Slowly Moriah reached up and slid one hand beneath his hair, cupping it around the back of his neck, drawing him closer. Before his lips could touch hers again, he jerked his head upward.

"I cannot—God help me!" His words came out constricted with pain.

She let go of him as if he had burned her and retreated a step back, her eyes wide.

"My lady—"

"No!" she cried softly, shaking her head. "No. I–I do not wish to hear it." With trembling fingers, she replaced a portion of the *palla* over her head until it again shielded her face.

Humiliated by her wanton behavior and despairing of his rejection, Moriah hurried down the stairs and to the dark road, barely cognizant of Aidan's footsteps echoing behind. What must he think of her? In all probability he thought her no better than Flavia. But she loved Aidan beyond reason and wanted no other. Surely that made the union he so solemnly denounced suitable? All this time she thought he returned her feelings—had been certain of it—but obviously she was mistaken. She felt hollow inside but not quite empty enough to be numb to the searing pain that stabbed her heart.

Aidan's hand on her sleeve halted her hasty retreat.

"My lady, you are going in the wrong direction," he said quietly.

She yanked her arm from his hold and whirled the other way, her footsteps swift. The walk up the hill was as silent as when they first set out, but uncomfortably so. When they reached the door to the garden, Moriah hurried to her *cubiculum* without once looking Aidan's way.

&

Throughout the next few days, when she did not dwell on her shameful experience with Aidan, Moriah thought of her nocturnal introduction to the Christian faith. She still had questions, especially concerning God's unconditional love, which Peter spoke of at the meeting. If this Most High God was truly One of such love, why then would He be averse to a union between Moriah and Aidan? She shook her head. It was only an excuse. Aidan had given her a tepid excuse because he personally wanted nothing to do with her. Now his distance made sense. Still, their kisses had made her feel so alive, so warm, awakening something deep within. And he had seemed to find pleasure in them, as well.

Frustrated, unable to concentrate, Moriah made numerous errors in her daily duties. Now that Lydia was gone and Moriah's management of the household was a permanent responsibility, she must see to it that everything ran smoothly, befitting the house of Dinoculus. When Flavia suddenly appeared, inviting Moriah to accompany her to the market, she agreed, glad for a temporary respite.

Aidan joined them, as was his task, and Flavia looked toward Moriah with an upraised brow. Moriah only shook her head, indicating she did not wish to discuss it. However, once they were secured in the privacy of Flavia's litter carried by six slaves with Aidan walking alongside them, Flavia spoke, her brows lifted in curiosity. "Why does your father's servant accompany us?"

Moriah kept her gaze focused on the hazy buildings as seen through the yellow veil of the litter. "Father thinks I should have a bodyguard."

"A bodyguard?"

Moriah nodded. "Father assigned me to Aidan's care shortly after those men from the alley tried to harm me."

"Really?" Flavia sat back among the silk cushions. "I

wonder if this means your father is tiring of Aidan." At Moriah's shrug and seeming indifference, she continued. "I've talked to my father. He's agreed to make your father an offer for Aidan."

Moriah turned her head sharply in Flavia's direction. "An offer?"

Flavia nodded, her eyes gleaming. "As you know, Aidan has piqued my interest for some time. He is so strong and handsome—like a Roman god. I'm certain he would more than know how to satisfy a woman."

Moriah felt sick when she thought of Aidan's fate at the hands of Flavia. His excuses would not hold up well against a woman of such power. He would be forced to yield or face severe punishment. Moriah's cheeks went hot as detailed pictures filled her mind of the two of them together. Flavia gave a mocking laugh.

"Why, Moriah, you blush! Such an innocent. It is time you discover the pleasures about which you've only heard from my lips." She moved closer, as though divulging a secret. "Servius would be the perfect partner to introduce you to such pleasures—I should know. I am certain he would forgive your childish behavior at the banquet, and I doubt he believes the rumor circulating about you."

Moriah wrinkled her brow. "Rumor?"

Flavia studied her closely, then shook her head. "Never mind. I should not have spoken."

Moriah's cheeks went hot, and she looked away. Her cowardice at the circus must have been publicized, or perhaps her escape from the banquet was now widely known, and as a result, many citizens probably thought her less than a true daughter of Rome.

"I do not like Servius Antonus," she explained and shuddered. "He frightens me."

Flavia laughed. "Oh, Moriah, you are such a child." She tilted her head and grew thoughtful. "Because our families have been friends for many years, perhaps after I tire of

Aidan, I will let you buy him back, if it pleases you. But I warn you, I do not expect that to happen for some time." She gave a lewd smile, making Moriah's stomach turn. Indeed, she felt physically ill.

When they reached the marketplace, the men carrying the litter lowered it. Moriah hastened to pull away the thin veil, anxious to escape its suddenly unbearable confines. The air was fragrant with cinnamon and other spices being sold nearby, and she took a deep breath.

Aidan reached out to assist her. The heat of his hand on hers made her tremble, and she quickly averted her gaze.

Flavia asked for Aidan's assistance, and he complied. To Moriah's chagrin, Flavia clasped his upper arm with both of her hands as she exited the litter, then pretended to stumble, moving closer to Aidan and letting her body brush his momentarily, suggestively, before she stepped away.

Disgusted, Moriah focused on a stall lined with baskets of cooing doves and pigeons. She watched as a man purchased a pair of doves, probably to offer as a sacrifice at one of the nearby temples.

Flavia chattered happily, visiting one stall after another, bartering with the tradesmen and adding to her collection of finery. Moriah silently followed, Aidan beside her.

"Behold!" Flavia lifted a whisper-thin piece of green silk and held it to her ample bosom. "Is it not perfect, Moriah?"

The tradesman, his brown face split in a huge smile, nodded enthusiastically. "You would surely rival all the goddesses of the universe by displaying your rare beauty in such a garment."

Flavia's brow winged upward at the glib remark. She looked down at the piece of transparent silk, then her eyes turned toward Aidan, a gleam lighting their depths. She smiled. "Yes. Yes, I think I may have need of this soon. What is your price?"

For the next few minutes the two bartered until Flavia walked away, satisfied, the green silk tucked under her arm.

Moriah wanted nothing more than to return home. Flavia

looked at her. "Are you not going to make a purchase, Moriah? Paulus has a birthday in two weeks, does he not?"

Moriah's eyes widened at Flavia's reminder. How could she have forgotten? Though she had no idea if Paulus would return by then, she hastened to a nearby stall selling amulets and charms and began eyeing its wares.

"Do you seek a potion, my lady?" the tradesman suggested with an avaricious grin. "Or perhaps an amulet to grant good fortune to its wearer?"

Moriah gave a slight shake of her head, trying to ignore the exuberant little man. A tiny jade figurine of an Abyssinian cat caught her attention, reminding her of her cat, Claudius, Paulus's long-ago present to her. She picked up the statuette, studying it with a critical eye, pleased to note its quality.

It was perfect. Special and sentimental—yet not so much so—a gift a woman would give to a man she loved as a brother. Of course, Moriah knew it was possible that Clophelius might agree to a match between her and Paulus, with or without her consent.

Hesitant, Moriah looked toward Aidan, who stood to the side of her a short distance away. He stared directly at her, his gaze tender.

The jade carving slipped from her suddenly nerveless fingers, hitting the flagstones with a sharp crack. The tradesman issued a loud groan.

Hurriedly, Moriah bent to retrieve the figurine, almost bumping heads with Aidan, who did the same. Simultaneously, they reached for the tiny statue. A powerful jolt, like nearby lightning, traveled through Moriah when his fingers brushed hers.

Startled, she withdrew her hand. Her head snapped up and her face went hot. Dark blue eyes filled with undisguised longing stared into hers an eternal moment, and Moriah drew a swift breath.

Flavia cleared her throat. Aidan quickly averted his gaze and picked up the jade cat, placing it in Moriah's hand. "It appears unharmed, my lady."

His low, unstable voice sent tremors of warmth through Moriah. Yet he did not look her way again.

Hastily, she stood and paid the hawker the exorbitant price he asked. Confused, she wanted only to leave this place and return to the house. There she could take time to dwell on what had happened if, indeed, anything had happened. Perhaps she had imagined the powerful connection she experienced with Aidan when she looked into his eyes—as well as the love she had seen there.

Once Moriah moved from the stall of the pleased tradesman, Flavia hissed, "Really, Moriah, you are so naive! Even when it comes to the purchasing of goods. Consider this. You could have bought that statue for half the price had you bartered, and likely you might have found it cheaper elsewhere."

Moriah barely listened, still shaken from her encounter with Aidan. Once they were within the privacy of the litter, Flavia thoughtfully studied Moriah.

"Or perhaps you are not as naive as I supposed. I saw what happened between you and your father's slave when you dropped that statue. A person would have to be blind not to have noticed. So tell me, Moriah, have you sought his pleasure?"

Remembering the passionate kiss she had shared with Aidan on the temple steps, Moriah felt her cheeks burn and hurriedly looked away. "Really, Flavia, you exasperate me! Does nothing else cross your mind?"

Flavia gave a coarse laugh. "What else is there, my friend?"

When Clophelius's house came into view, Moriah was glad. Yet once they walked through the door, her relief metamorphosed into burgeoning disquiet.

Servius Antonus strode from the *bibliotheca,* obviously having just visited Clophelius. A gleam entered his eyes when he caught sight of them. "Greetings, Moriah. Flavia." He gave a curt nod toward the blond, who quickly made her farewells and left as though she had received some sort of signal from the man.

Wary, Moriah appraised the unwanted guest.

He focused his attention on her, his gaze roaming her form before returning to her face in the same manner he always ogled her. "I have petitioned your father. Soon, Moriah, you will be mine."

"Yours?" Her voice came out hoarse.

"My wife."

Moriah's eyes grew wide in disbelief. Revulsion filled her at the thought. How could Clophelius betray her like this? And what of Paulus?

She looked beyond Servius's shoulder, searching out Aidan. He stood at the portal, his expression one of helpless frustration. Clearly he was against the match, and that thought gave Moriah a measure of comfort. Though he evidently wanted no deeper relationship with her, perhaps he would speak to Clophelius on her behalf since Paulus was not here to do so. Clophelius regarded Aidan highly. He might listen to him.

"Tomorrow night, Moriah," Servius murmured seductively. Reaching for her fingers, he trapped them.

She snatched her hand from his sweaty grasp and looked at him, unable to hide her aversion.

He frowned, then smiled stiffly. "Tomorrow night shall be the start of our life together."

nine

Moriah stepped inside the *bibliotheca,* smoothing her clammy hands down the sides of her *stola*. She had decided to approach Clophelius herself rather than ask Aidan to do so. There was no telling how the master of the house would respond, and she did not wish to put Aidan in a position that might lose him favor.

Clophelius looked up from the scroll on which he was writing, his brows raised in surprise. "You wish to speak with me?"

In all the years she had been raised in his household, Moriah had never dared enter his presence unless summoned. In the past month, she had done so twice. Clearing her throat, she began, "I am greatly disturbed by the news Servius Antonus shared with me upon my return from the market."

Clophelius frowned and straightened. "Go on," he said formidably.

Moriah swallowed past the lump in her throat, her gaze leaving his stern face and focusing on the statue of Apollo sitting in a nook of the room. Even paralyzed, Clophelius had the ability to frighten her.

"He told me that you have given consent to a match between us." Just saying the words left a bitter taste in her mouth.

"And if I have?"

Moriah's heart plummeted at his detached tone. "I do not think you would do such a thing," she whispered, her wide gaze going to his at the mounting possibility that it was so, and Servius had, indeed, been telling the truth. "Before Mother died, you promised her that you would care for me—she told me this."

"I have not broken my vow!" His eyes burned with anger. "Dare you deny it?"

"No," she said quickly. "You have given me the best of everything, though I am not your true daughter. For that, I am grateful."

Clophelius nodded, satisfied. "You have spoken well." He paused, studying her as she picked at the folds of her *stola*. She made a deliberate effort to cease her nervous movements.

"I have not given my final word on the match," he said, "regardless of what Antonus has told you. True, he is a man of power, but I hold a measure of the same. However, consider this. Servius Antonus is a man of great wealth. His cousin recently married a man distantly related to the emperor, and Servius himself is related to Senator Valerius."

When he paused, Moriah nodded for him to go on, the great beast of dread looming over her.

"Paulus informed me that you are aware of your unfortunate parentage. It has come to light for others, as well. Servius is willing to overlook the matter since he believes it only a rumor. A match to him would be in the best interest for you. He will soon journey to his villa in Naples. There is a distinct possibility that the truth has reached the ear of Nero, and a marriage to Servius Antonus may be an acceptable way to protect you and remove you from Rome—"

"Protect me?" Moriah broke in. "How can marrying such a vile man as Servius be of any protection to me?"

"Silence, Woman! I do not care for your insolent tongue." When Moriah submissively dropped her gaze, Clophelius continued. "It is true that Servius has certain. . .vices, but they are no different from any other Roman's. Consider this as well, Moriah. He is a powerful citizen of enormous influence. As his wife, you would want for nothing."

Miserable, she studied the mosaic tiles. "And what of Paulus? Surely he could offer me any protection I might need?"

At her faint words, Clophelius slammed the scroll down, hitting the edge of the marble table. The rolled parchment clattered to the floor. Moriah winced but dared not look up.

"So, Paulus told you of his plans, though I distinctly

remember telling him not to do so. How dare he defy me a second time! First, by telling you the truth about your parentage and now this. I am still head of this household—a fact that seems to have escaped his knowledge as well as yours!"

Despair flooded Moriah. There was nothing more to be said. She had tried and failed. With bowed head, she clasped her hands in front of her. "If there is nothing more, I will take your leave."

Clophelius relaxed, obviously pacified by her sudden obeisance. "Antonus spoke out of turn. I never agreed to a match on the morrow." He continued to study her. "Perhaps I shall give you a short time to grow accustomed to the idea."

Moriah stared, baffled that he would consider her feelings. "I–I would be grateful for such an action on my behalf. Though I know I could never grow to love him."

"Love?" Clophelius scoffed. "Neither did I love Lydia when first we exchanged wafers at the marriage ceremony. Yet I came to regard her fondly as the years passed, though she bore me no heir. It was because of my regard for her that I agreed to her supplication to raise you as a member of this household."

Moriah remained silent, uncertain how to respond. Never had Clophelius spoken to her in such an open manner.

"I made a promise to Lydia to see to your welfare, and I intend to keep my vow. You cannot help what your parents were, I suppose," he added thoughtfully, rubbing his chin.

Something in her expression at the reference to her parents must have alarmed him, for he straightened, his face sober. "You must never speak of the matter, Moriah. Forget what Paulus told you. You are a Roman. Even now, the fledgling of truth that has hatched can sprout wings no longer accepted as rumor, which in turn could become the bane of our existence. Lately Nero has not taken kindly to those who call themselves Christians." He said the last as though the word were leprous. "I do not wish it to appear that I am on the opposing side."

"I shall do as you ask," Moriah said quietly, though she did not fully understand all he said about fledglings of truth hatching and sprouting wings and rumors. She would dwell on it another time. Only one thing mattered to her at the moment. She gathered courage. "And as to the matter of Servius?"

Clophelius waved his hand in barely concealed annoyance, obviously weary of the subject. "I shall think more on the matter, as I have stated. Perhaps there is another way. Then again, perhaps not."

Moriah was grateful for any reprieve, however uncertain. Paulus might soon return and could then talk to Clophelius and get him to realize that it would be a mistake to match Moriah to Servius. All was not lost. So much could happen between now and then.

"You may go." Clophelius leaned over and picked up the discarded scroll from the floor. Frowning, he began to peruse it.

Summarily dismissed, Moriah strode to her *cubiculum*, hopeful that something could be done before it was too late.

❧

Listening to the gentle melody Sinista produced as she whisked her fingers over the strings of the cithara, Moriah stood beside the couch on her enclosed terrace and looked out at the city of Rome, preparing to bed for the night.

The tradesmen who sold their wares in the marketplace had gone. Carts and wagons would rumble down the thoroughfares once darkness had completely fallen and the ban was lifted on four-wheeled conveyances in the city. In the valley below, a group of richly dressed citizens entered a temple, leading an ox up the stairs. Nearby, a group of beggar children combed the ground for scraps of food, a lost coin—anything they could find.

In the west, thick clouds blushed crimson, as though ashamed of the city they watched, and produced a bold backdrop of color against the mammoth stone temples that soared to the sky in seeming defiance. A small group of expensively dressed citizens hurried past, evidently late to wherever they journeyed from what Moriah could understand of their quarrel heard faintly from her position at the lattice window. In all directions she looked, someone seemed to be going somewhere, doing something. The sight made her restless, and she turned her back to it. Suddenly she found the lilting music irritating.

"You may go," Moriah told the slave. "And tell Hermes to send loaves of bread to those children outside."

Sinista stood with her instrument, bowed, and hurried away. Moriah again faced the window, wishing she could order feelings of restlessness and discontent to go as well and be as quickly obeyed. She let out a weary sigh.

If only Aidan cared. . .or Clophelius changed his mind. . .or Servius found another victim. If only she belonged to someone who loved her. To someone she, in turn, could love.

The people below appeared assured, striding boldly to their destinations, all in the company of those whom it appeared they were satisfied to be with. Even the beggar children stayed close, drawing comfort from one another's presence.

Moriah lifted tear-glazed eyes to the darkening sky. Dim pinpoints of stars were becoming visible, clusters and clusters of them. Did any of them feel lonely in their existence though they were surrounded by thousands of others?

She blew out an exasperated breath. What foolishness! Stars had no feelings. Only people did. And Moriah felt the loneliness stronger tonight than in all her twenty-two years on the earth. Aidan rejected her love. Deborah, though attentive as always, seemed to have emotionally distanced herself from Moriah since their conversation on this terrace. Paulus was in Antium, and she rarely saw him when he was in Rome because of his imperial duties. And if Clophelius decreed it, she was to marry a man whom she despised. Twice this week, Servius had come to the house to speak with Clophelius. On the first occasion he left angered; today he departed with a satisfied smirk, the reason for which Moriah feared would bode her ill.

A tear rolled down her cheek. She dashed it away impatiently and wove her fingers through the lattice window, gripping it until her knuckles turned white. Was she forever doomed to a life of unhappiness?

Memory of the night she attended the Christian meeting floated to her with the warm breeze. The people there belonged, knit together as one family. She remembered what the apostle Peter spoke about Jesus, the One who called Himself the Christ. The Anointed One. And though she did not fully understand everything the apostle had said that night, Moriah knew what she must do. What she suddenly wanted to do.

Looking up at the stars in the dusky purple twilight, she dashed any remaining tears from her eyes. Her stance was almost defiant, though within she trembled.

"God of Aidan and others who call themselves Christians, I do not know You. I do not understand Your teachings or Your ways. They are so foreign to all I've been taught as a Roman." She lowered her lashes and bit the inside corner of her mouth, trying to frame her words. She did not want to make this God angry.

"I am aware that You must be real, having witnessed the strong faith and love of Your people and having heard the message Your disciples preached." Moriah paused, needing to swallow over the sudden lump that inexplicably rose to her throat. More tears blurred her vision.

"And if You will allow it," she whispered, "I wish to belong to Your family. I–I realize it was my father who put You to death on the cross. But if You will pardon that and not hold it against me. . ."

She fell to her knees, the power of her tightly held emotions making her body tremble. Desperately she clutched the lattices and lifted her gaze toward the violet sky. "God of the Christians—Jesus the *Christus*—I'm truly sorry for what my father did. Rufus said that You forgave both Peter for his betrayal and Paul for his persecution of Your people and accepted them into Your family. And that You accepted my parents, as well. If this is so, then I also wish to know You.

I wish for You to be my God."

Moriah released the window and collapsed to the floor. Fierce emotion wracked her body. Hot tears rushed between her clenched eyelids, and she thought she might die from the sensations tearing through her.

Why should this God accept her—a pagan, a Roman, the daughter of the man who had put Him to death? Why should He forgive her or her father?

As Moriah quieted, something peculiar happened. Soothing warmth began to course through her midregion, spreading its glow throughout her insides like a growing flame until she felt immersed in the most astounding peace. It was as though invisible arms wrapped themselves around her, cradling her, loving her.

Assuring her that she now belonged.

Astonished, Moriah raised herself up on one hand and lifted her face heavenward. "You love me," she whispered. A faint smile lifted the corners of her mouth as she basked in the warmth of God's love and peace for the first time. She would have liked nothing better than to lie there and soak up the blissful feeling for an eternity, but Moriah was convinced there was something more she must do.

Rising to a kneeling position, Moriah lifted her arms and declared a solemn oath to the heavens. "From this day forward, Most High God, I pledge to You my loyalty and my life. I vow to serve You above all other gods, for now I know that You are the One True God. And to Your Son, Jesus the *Christus,* I give all that I am. Do with me as You will, my Lord and my God."

A dove cooed in the distance, the sound soothing in the tranquil room. From afar, Moriah thought she discerned myriad voices lifted in beautiful chorus. The faint singing grew steadily in volume and was unlike anything she had previously heard, saturating her with such hope and joy that she wished she could also lift her voice in praise. Yet she could not utter a sound, her bewilderment was so great.

She continued to gaze at the stars seen beyond the openings of the lattice window. They appeared to shine more brightly than they had moments ago. Much too quickly, the singing faded until it disappeared altogether, and only the gentle warbling of the dove remained.

Awed, Moriah continued to look to the heavens, certain she would never forget this night.

෧

His mind echoing the abysmal words that had spilled from Clophelius's mouth, Aidan helped another slave tend the master. Moriah to wed Servius Antonus? Was Clophelius mad? The thought of her in the man's clutches was a torment too horrific to bear.

Servius had power. For that reason alone, Aidan was certain Clophelius had agreed to the match. Clophelius was thinking only of what a man like Servius could accomplish for him, with little regard for Moriah's welfare. How could he do such a thing to his only child—true daughter or no?

Barely refraining from digging the strigil deep into his master's back and taking off a layer of skin, Aidan completed the task, wishing to escape to the garden to pray. Lately his flesh warred with his spirit a great deal. He needed the armor of prayer to fight his base nature that often sought to overpower him.

Yet Clophelius was in high spirits tonight, wanting nothing more than to bask in the steaming waters and gloat about the fine match he had made for Moriah. Aidan clenched his teeth, striving for self-control as Clophelius congratulated himself yet another time and continued his one-man eulogy.

"She cannot yet see the good in such a union," he said, "and it is true that Lydia disliked the man. But a woman's thoughts are of little consequence in such matters. I deem what is best, and it is best they marry." He grew thoughtful. "I was almost penalized and required to pay a fine because Moriah had not married by the age of twenty. I should have matched her when she came of age at twelve. Yet Lydia was fond of the girl and wanted her close. As ill as Lydia was, I chose to give her whatever comfort I could by granting her Moriah's companionship. . . . Yet perhaps I erred in that respect."

He sighed and grew sober. "The years pass swiftly. Moriah's beauty will soon fade, and she will grow too old for a decent match. It is time she was wed. Tomorrow, I will announce my decision to both of them."

Surprised, Aidan stopped scraping oil from Clophelius's back, then slowly resumed his task. It was not too late? The announcement had not yet been made?

"Demas, bring more wine!" Clophelius ordered the other servant in the room and tipped his goblet upside-down to show it was empty. "How am I to celebrate without wine?"

The wiry man hurried out, and Clophelius again started to congratulate himself on the match. His words were assured, yet his manner was not. He was more tense than usual, and his smiles seemed false. Aidan couldn't be certain, but it didn't appear as though Clophelius was convinced he was embarking on the right course. Perhaps Aidan should speak. He had never interrupted one of the master's personal monologues before, indeed he had not spoken unless first addressed. But Moriah's future was at stake, and Clophelius did favor Aidan. Relying on that knowledge and mustering his courage, Aidan cleared his throat.

"Master, if I may speak?"

Clophelius seemed surprised but gave a curt nod. "Speak then."

"As patriarch of this household, you are a wise man and astute in your dealings. Your mind is quick and sharp. All who know you respect your views and esteem you highly, including our emperor."

"You speak well," Clophelius said with a smile. "Go on."

Aidan hesitated, knowing he was about to put his head on the block. Would Clophelius spare the sword or decimate him? "I am but a slave. Yet in my role as a slave, I see and hear things of which you may not be aware."

Clophelius frowned. "Such as?"

My God, continue to grant me favor, Aidan silently petitioned. He forced his strokes with the strigil to remain steady. "I have privately spoken with the servants of Servius Antonus in the marketplace. They have shared with me the disturbing news that late at night in his home Antonus oftentimes goes into a trance and emerges from it violent, as though he were possessed by some powerful evil. He beat his last lover within an inch of her life and has harmed others, as well." Aidan knew that Servius also beat his servants, but such a statement would not faze his master, who occasionally gave the order for the same to be done with his slaves. Aidan had never been beaten while in this household. At Clophelius's brooding silence, he wondered if that were about to change.

"Ungrateful servants are apt to spread lies concerning their masters," Clophelius said at last, and Aidan's heart plummeted.

"Yes, Master, it is so."

Clophelius looked over his shoulder, his manner reflective. "However, I am aware that you are not one to spread vicious rumors, Aidan. Nor do you speak falsehoods. Well you have served me these many years, and I prefer you above all others in my household." He nodded slowly as though in deep thought. "I will consider your words. Leave me and tell Kryton to come. I desire to quit this bath. And where is that worthless slave with my wine? I could have retrieved it more quickly had I crawled on my belly to get it."

Aidan laid the strigil on a nearby table and gave a short bow. "I shall look into it, my lord."

With no other duties required of him for the night, Aidan left the room. Approaching the young slave carrying the vessel of the master's wine, Aidan cautioned him to hurry and continued through the colonnaded walkway, his mind a jumble of thoughts.

He was pleased Clophelius had agreed to ponder the matter of Moriah's marriage further. Yet even if the master were to side in her favor and deny Servius, Clophelius would then likely match her to Centurion Paulus Seneca. And though Paulus was a fine man who obviously cared for Moriah, the thought of her becoming his wife caused Aidan's heart to grow as heavy as an amphora laden to the brim with olive oil.

As it frequently was apt to do, his mind returned to the night he and Moriah had escaped the soldiers and embraced on the temple stairs. How it had pained Aidan to see the despair in her eyes when she pleaded with him to admit he loved her. The words had risen to his throat, begging release. Yet in the instant before he opened his mouth to speak, Aidan realized that to do so would not change matters.

Even if his role were not that of a slave and she were not the daughter of a patrician, he had recently learned through the teaching of one of the disciples that he could not join with a woman who did not share the faith. He could not be un-equally yoked with an unbeliever. Yet that knowledge did not remove the feelings for her that smoldered in his heart.

"Oh Lord, my God, help me," Aidan moaned as he sank to the ground inside the arbor and clasped his hands together on the stone bench. He lowered his head to them, his heart raw from the frequent wounds of defeat and hopelessness. "I am but a man, and she is everything I wish for in a wife. I choose to do Your will, Lord. Yet my flesh is so very weak. I cannot stop thinking of her, dreaming of her. She invades my every waking thought when she's not in my presence, and when I sleep at night, I wish for her beside me. When I am with her, I look upon her countenance, though it is forbidden to do so, and foolishly hope for things that cannot be. Give me strength to resist wicked inducements, Lord, and to walk in the path You have set before me. It would almost be better were she to marry Centurion Seneca and leave this place, so that the daily temptation to take her in my arms is removed."

The words were bitter like gall, but Aidan forced them out. "If a match is to be made, let my master choose Centurion Seneca for my lady's husband." His eyes closed. "And help me, Lord, to accept what can never be."

Aidan remained kneeling though his words ceased, cut off as they were by the pain blocking his throat. Usually after prayer, he felt a surge of inner strength equip him. But tonight he felt nothing but loss and a portent of danger.

Danger?

He raised his head, alert, and noticed something he had not formerly detected. The acrid smell of smoke filled his nostrils as though a bonfire had been lit beyond the garden wall. Before he could investigate further, light footsteps on the path hurried toward him. He tensed.

"Aidan?"

Slowly he stood to his feet and turned, his manner wary.

"I wish to speak with you," Moriah said, an undercurrent of excitement ringing in her voice. The moon in the hazy sky was almost full, but its light was blocked from the branches of a nearby olive tree. Still Aidan felt as though he could discern every nuance of expression on the face so dear to him.

"I am at your disposal, my lady."

She looked away to the garden wall. "Not here. Let us walk."

He hesitated. His unstable emotions were too near the surface for him to spend much time in her presence. To do so could very well prove dangerous. Just standing near her, he fought the strong impulse to take her in his arms.

"It is late," he said quietly. "If someone sees us together, it may not go well for either of us."

"Father was in unusual spirits tonight and drank quite heavily of the vine. He's in deep slumber, and I do not fear the others. Nor should you. Come, Aidan. What I have to say is of importance, I assure you."

Moriah began to walk, and Aidan did likewise, the soft clack of his sandals keeping time with hers. As they strolled closer to the door in the wall, muted shouts could be heard in the distance—obviously Romans partaking in some sort of revelry.

"Aidan, there is something I wish to tell you. Something I wish to share."

Suddenly nervous, uncertain how he would react, Moriah

stopped and reached for a flower growing on a vine along the high wall. She snapped the stem and brought the white blossom to her nose, appreciatively inhaling its sweet fragrance. The strong scent of jasmine surrounded them, and Moriah sensed Aidan stiffen beside her.

"It is my favorite scent," she explained, lifting her head. Her eyes sought his in the dim light. "I had a merchant create the perfume especially for me because I liked the scent so well, even more so than roses."

Moriah's cheeks burned. Here she stood babbling about flowers and perfumes, when to be this close to him what she really wanted was to cradle his strong jaw in her hands. To take a step closer and press her lips to his.

Turning abruptly, she put a short amount of distance between them. Reminding herself of why she'd sought him out, Moriah faced him once again. "I digress. You see, Aidan, something happened tonight. Something so astounding and powerful I scarcely know how to describe it. Nonetheless, I question if you would believe me if I were to find the words to share with you. How to explain?" She shook her head, searching for a solid starting point. "Perhaps by telling you this: I understand now what you told me during our nightly discussions, here, in the garden—"

"My lady!" Deborah's shrill voice shattered the air, and Moriah gave a startled little jump. Bare feet slapped the path in a mad run. "My lady, where are you?" Deborah cried again, desperation coating her words.

Moriah shot an anxious glance toward Aidan before responding. "Here, Deborah! Near the door in the wall."

The running came louder until Deborah stood before them, her hair tangled and flowing past her waist. Her coal black eyes were round. Even in the scant light in which they stood, her fear was tangible.

"My lady, Rome burns!"

"Burns?"

Deborah pointed toward the citrus trees near the house.

Above their leafy canopies, the nighttime sky held an ominous red glow Moriah had not noticed before. Her eyes widened.

"Rome!" Deborah gasped. "The city is on fire!"

"Father must be told," Moriah said in a barely audible voice. She looked Aidan's way.

Even in the dark, he seemed to sense her appeal and nodded. "I will come with you."

Together they hurried to Clophelius's *cubiculum*. Kryton jumped up from a pallet near the door. Seeing Moriah, followed by Deborah and Aidan, he lowered his weapon, evidently puzzled by their presence at the master's bedchamber this time of night.

Moriah did not spare him a second glance but pulled away the curtain and hurried inside. "Father, awaken! It is most urgent I speak with you."

Groaning met her pleas followed by a string of curses. "Why have you interrupted my slumber? What brings you here at this forsaken hour?"

"Rome's on fire!" Moriah exclaimed. "You must arise quickly."

Clophelius pushed himself up to a sitting position while Deborah lit a taper. The added light was hardly necessary. Clophelius's window faced the Aventine Hill, and a yellow glow covered the thin drape separating the bed from his balcony. Clophelius nodded for Aidan to move the curtain aside.

Moriah gasped and put her hand to the wall. She watched in stunned silence as leaping flames in the distance engulfed countless buildings in the valley. There seemed no order to the madness.

"By all that is sacred, he's done it," Clophelius rasped in horror.

Moriah looked at him sharply. "Who?"

Clophelius closed his eyes. For a moment, Moriah did not think he would answer her faint query. "Senator Valerius spoke of how Nero has complained he could not be expected to write prose comparable to Homer if he could not actually see a fire overtake a city. Valerius told me that Nero has been secretive of late, as though he were planning something, but surely. . .surely he would not order an incident as monstrous as this."

"You must be mistaken," Moriah quickly inserted, alarmed by his treasonous words. She did not trust all the slaves in the household and knew some were not as loyal as they pretended. "Likely your slumber has dulled your clarity of mind. Nero has a duty to his people. He would not cause harm to those who revere him as leader. Who then would be left to honor him?" After she uttered the last words, Moriah realized that in her fear, she had spoken out of turn. Yet Clophelius seemed not to notice.

He released a long, shaky breath. "Yes. Yes, you are right. Doubtless, shock clouded my logic for a moment. Mayhap it is only one of many fires that occasionally erupt in the city. Likely vandals have caused it. We are far enough away. I am certain it will be contained soon."

Yet while Moriah watched the greedy flames race through the valley, she knew this was like no fire Rome had ever seen.

ten

From the confines of the house, Moriah viewed the frenzied commotion below, oblivious to the passage of time. She had long since left Clophelius's *cubiculum* and hurried to the terrace of her own room, now lit up by the glow of distant fires.

Everywhere she looked, terrified people ran through the twisted, narrow streets. Some toted personal possessions on their backs. Women carried crying babies in their arms, while older children hurried in their parents' footsteps.

Flames had spread to other parts of the city as the fire continued to grow. How long had it burned? Why did it spread so quickly? A blaze of such magnitude must have started some time ago. Why had she heard nothing of it?

Moriah clutched the lattice window until the wooden strips bit into her fingers. The urgency to leave and join the teeming crowd was overpowering.

Hearing a commotion outside her room, Moriah hurried to the atrium to investigate. Clophelius reclined on his couch, now dressed, his bodyguard standing behind him. Aidan stood a few feet away. Yet it was on the servant Clophelius sent out earlier to gather news that Moriah focused her attention. Trembling, the wiry young man fell to his knees at his master's feet, obviously having run a great distance.

"Well, Demas?" Clophelius prompted impatiently. "Speak!"

"They say the fires broke out near the circus some time ago," the slave panted, his dark eyes fearful. "There are many. A strong wind carries the flames, and they are out of control—spreading like serpents gone mad, with no rhyme or reason. The gods are angry! Vulcan has unleashed his wrath on us! Rome will perish. We will all perish!" he cried, lifting his hands in frightened supplication toward the heavens.

"Enough!" Clophelius motioned the frightened man away with a disgusted flick of his hand. He turned his gaze toward Moriah and studied her, as though trying to reach a decision, then gave a swift nod and focused on Aidan. "I wish to speak with you in the *bibliotheca*. Kryton, Paltheus, assist me."

The bodyguard and another slave hurried to lift Clophelius's couch and carry him to the library. Forgetting they were in the company of others, Moriah put a hand to Aidan's arm before he could follow.

"What is happening?" she implored, though it was a foolish question. Obviously he didn't have the answer any more than she did.

"I don't know, my lady." His eyes tried to offer a measure of reassurance, as did his tone. "But God will take care of us. Of that, I'm certain."

Anxious, Moriah watched him enter the *bibliotheca*. She wished her newfound faith were as strong as Aidan's.

૨ð

Aidan waited for his master to speak. Clophelius clasped his hands in front of him on the couch and stared at them a moment before looking up at Aidan, who stood across from him.

"I have arrived at a decision." He turned to Kryton. "Bring papyrus and a reed," he told the man at his elbow. "Paltheus, bring a table."

Both slaves turned to retrieve the needed articles.

"I am uncertain what the future holds, Aidan, but I made a vow to see to Moriah's protection. I intend to honor that vow despite the recent opposition toward me by those in my own household."

He sighed and unclasped his hands. "You are to take Moriah out of the city and find a place of refuge. I doubt the fire will reach this hill. But if it should happen, at least Moriah will be safe, and I will have honored my promise to Lydia. Afterward, if all is well, you are to bring her back so that she may then marry the man I have chosen for her."

Aidan tried to school his features to remain impassive. "As

you wish, my lord. Will you not leave the city, as well?"

Clophelius shook his head, a wry tilt to his lips. "I am a paralyzed old man. I have not left this house in the eight years since the accident, and I will not leave it now. If death is to overtake me, then let it be in the comfort of my personal surroundings."

He leaned back against the tilted head of the couch, studying Aidan. "You have been a good slave. Loyal. Subservient. I am well pleased with your service to me these many years."

A sudden thought reared its head, causing Aidan discomfort. Clophelius had mentioned his pleasure with Aidan's service, yet what of Aidan's service to his true Master? In the past, fear of being discovered had kept Aidan's tongue still. Now that he was leaving Clophelius's presence, perhaps never to see his master again, should he not try to share the message of the gospel? Clophelius had shown him a measure of kindness, more so than to any of the other slaves. If the master were to die this night, did he not first deserve to hear the truth undistorted by wicked rumor? He might listen to Aidan, since he'd done so before.

"Master, before we part, I have a matter I wish to discuss with you." He said the words hesitantly, knowing if he were wrong in his assumptions, it could cost his friends danger or perhaps even Aidan his life.

One gray brow winged upward in surprise. "You may speak in a moment, Aidan. But first I have something more I wish to say."

⁂

Moriah restlessly paced her *cubiculum*. She tried to ignore Sinista's sniffles in between frequent glances to the window and what she could see of the city beyond.

"Will we burn, my lady?" the slave cried. "Is this truly the end?"

"I have a sister who lives on the Esquiline Hill," Sahara said solemnly to no one in particular as she stood on the terrace and stared at the conflagration overtaking the city. "She is slave to a merchant who lives there."

Moriah's fingernails dug into her palms. The fright in her servants' voices added fuel to her own worries. She had no idea what to tell these women. How could one think when the mouth of Hades had opened wide to swallow them whole?

"My lady?"

Relieved, Moriah turned at the welcome sound of Aidan's voice. The maids cast him a glance, then looked back to the fires. Under such circumstances, evidently no one thought twice of his presence in her bedchamber. "Yes?"

"I have been ordered to take you out of the city. We shall leave at once. I will wait for you in the atrium."

"Very well." She was relieved to hear they would at last engage in a course of action rather than stay and do nothing. Her gaze swept her room. She felt as though it was the last time she would look upon its frescoed walls. She would never return.

Once Aidan left, Moriah faced the women who had served her all her life. Their slanted dark eyes shone luminous with fear. "You must also leave," Moriah stated firmly. "Go. While you have the chance."

They looked between themselves in uncertainty. "My lady?" Sinista asked, a tremor in her husky voice as she turned to Moriah again.

"You belong to me and I may do as I wish concerning you. I choose to set you free," Moriah explained. "Leave Rome and find refuge before it's too late."

Sinista's kohled eyes grew large and her mouth went slack. She fell to her knees and grabbed Moriah's hand, kissing it. "Oh, my lady, thank you," she sobbed.

Moriah's throat tightened, and she gently removed her hand from the woman's tight grip. "Go, Sinista. You must both go—quickly."

The two women gave Moriah one last heartfelt glance before exiting the room, almost running into Deborah as she hurried inside.

Moriah solemnly regarded her friend. "I cannot grant you the freedom to go, as I have done to my servants, since I know you are already free. Before she died, Lydia told me that it was by your own choice you stayed on the night you brought me to this house when I was an infant. She did not buy you. Yet I am ashamed to say, even if you were a slave, I am not certain I could grant you your freedom. You are very dear to me." Moriah lifted her chin and fought the tears that wanted to come.

Deborah took Moriah's cold hand in hers and gazed up at her with earnest eyes. "My lady, I will not leave your side for as long as you wish me to stay. I was but twelve when I brought you to this house, but I often have thought of you as my own."

Moriah resisted the urge to lay her head against Deborah's small shoulder as she had done when she was a child. Instead she squeezed her hand. "I cannot explain, but I feel as if I will never return."

"My lady?" Deborah's confusion was evident. "I doubt the fire will reach the house since it sits so high on the hill. The master is merely exercising caution."

Moriah gave a vague nod, though she felt her belief went much deeper than whether the house survived or not. Already it was as though a part of her had disassociated itself from these surroundings, and they seemed alien.

She did not belong here.

She shook her head slightly, breaking away from such peculiar thoughts, concentrating on the present. "Aidan is taking me out of the city. Will you come with us, Deborah?"

A spark of something resembling anger momentarily lit the Jewess's eyes, puzzling Moriah, but Deborah nodded. "I will come."

Once more, Moriah glanced over the room, her gaze landing on a marble table. A carved box containing her most prized pieces of jewelry caught her eye. She grabbed the small silver and ivory chest, then quickly turned, the folds of her *stola* swaying with the movement. "Let us depart from this place."

Though outwardly calm, Moriah could not quell the mounting apprehension that grew stronger with each passing moment. Together they moved toward the atrium.

Clophelius reclined on his couch near the *impluvium,* staring down into the rectangular basin containing rainwater captured from an opening in the ceiling, put there for that purpose. The black water shimmered in the light of a torch burning nearby. Upon hearing their hurried approach, he looked up. The events of the past hours had chiseled deep lines across his forehead, making him look older and less threatening.

"Father," Moriah began, uncertain what to say. Would she ever see him again? "Come with us."

At her quiet request, a softening touched the pale eyes, and she thought he might relent. But he shook his head. "As I told Aidan, I have stayed within these walls all the years following the accident that took the strength from my legs. Here is where I choose to remain." His gaze returned to the *impluvium.* "This will pass, if the gods will it. When things are as they were, Aidan will bring you home."

Moriah stared. Surely Clophelius did not imagine Rome could survive. The acrid smell of smoke had grown stronger. There was no telling what would greet her eyes once they walked beyond the door.

Moriah glanced at Aidan, who watched from his place beside a column. As though he read her mind, he cleared his throat. "We should go, my lady. Before the way becomes blocked."

She nodded and once more looked to the huddled figure reclining in front of her. The urge to reach out, to offer some sort of good-bye, was overpowering, and her hand rested on his shoulder. "Farewell, Father."

Momentary surprise crossed his haggard features. He lifted his plump hand to cover her slim one briefly, then dropped his arm back to the couch and looked away.

Blinking back sudden tears, Moriah turned and moved with Aidan and Deborah toward the outer door.

❧

A strong wind pushed against Aidan as he exited the house. He broke away from the women and moved down the first few steps of the hill as if in a stupor. From Clophelius's balcony, it had been impossible to see the full scope of destruction. Aidan had heard the fearful words of the slave Demas, but it had not prepared him for this. From his vantage point, facing the heart of the city, he could see clearly. Too clearly. Everywhere fires burned. To the left, the right, beyond, beneath—this was obviously caused by more than one fire. This was madness!

Huge tongues of flame outlined the dark night, destroying everything in its path like some many-headed monster bent on exacting revenge. A woman screamed as a man was inadvertently pushed into the fiery conflagration and one of the beast's heads greedily consumed him. To the right, a soldier recklessly drove his chariot from the heart of the writhing yellow monster, almost running down those who strayed in his path. Hordes of people swarmed the narrow streets. Screams pierced the night, discernable over the constant roar of the beast unleashed upon them. Looters, seemingly oblivious to the danger, sped through the streets, raiding temples, grabbing anything of value.

Moriah hurried down the stairs toward Aidan, her frightened gaze seeking his as she put a clammy hand to his arm. He looked at her, though he had no idea what to say. What reassurances could he offer when it appeared as if there were none to give?

The flickering glow from the firelight shone clearly in her anxious eyes, outlined her tense features, played itself over her white *stola,* danced in her dark hair. The illusion caused it to look as though Moriah were being engulfed in the flames, and a pain such as Aidan had never known pierced his heart.

He would not let her fall victim to this! But what could he do? The roads were congested with traffic, and they might not make it out of the city in time. Sudden memory flashed through his mind, and silently he thanked God for the answer. "Come. I know of a way out."

He took hold of her arm, and they moved as quickly as they

could down the hill and into the valley. Deborah followed.

The throng was moving too slowly, shoulder to shoulder as they were. Aidan led the women toward a nearby alley, trying to avoid the frantic crowd as they shoved one another. Some fell onto the streets. A grizzled man ran by pushing a hand-held cart containing what looked like all of his worldly goods. A barefoot woman in night garments rushed past, frantically pulling at handfuls of her loose hair and screaming, "The gods are angry! We shall all perish! There is no hope!"

Feeling as if, indeed, the world were ending, Moriah continued to clutch her small box to her breast with one hand and moved with Aidan as he pulled her along street after street and deeper into the heart of the city. Here the tall narrow buildings were of mud brick and wood, the *insulae* of the poor.

They turned a corner and reached a flaming labyrinth of buildings. Moriah's burning lungs felt as if they might explode from their endless run and the thick black smoke surrounding them. Heat more intense than anything previously experienced threatened to bake her skin. They turned another corner and came against a towering wall of flame. Moriah felt as though she were entering a fiery furnace. Aidan retraced his steps to another street. Flames shot up from the buildings to the sky on one side, yet the way was clear. Panicked but weary, Moriah stumbled to a stop. Harsh coughs racked her body.

"I can go no farther," she rasped, trying to make her voice heard above the shouts and the crackling fire. She gripped his arm more tightly. "Please! I think we must be going the wrong way. You are taking us into the heart of the fire!"

Rivulets of sweat trickled down his soot-streaked face, and his eyes burned with determination. "My lady, through that archway and around the corner down another street lies a home with its own entrance to the catacombs. If we can reach it, we can leave Rome underground."

"Underground? Through the *Cloaca Maxima?*" Deborah's black eyes filled with distrust.

"No, not through the sewers. I know of a tunnel away from

the drains. There is no water there."

"Surely we will suffocate," Deborah argued loudly. "How can we be certain he truly knows the way and we will not be forever lost inside the bowels of the earth? My lady, let us return to *Via Appia* and follow the crowd to the gate! For there we will surely find safety."

"I can find the way," Aidan replied. His gaze swept to Moriah, and his eyes were steady. "God will lead us. Of this I am certain."

Terror clutched Moriah at the thought of going below the earth, but she nodded, anxious to escape the searing heat. Anything would be better than this!

Aidan led them past two multistoried buildings towering on either side of the street. Consumed by fire, the *insulae* on their left threatened to topple to the ground and throw flaming wood on their heads at any moment.

"Make haste, my lady," Aidan instructed, pulling on her arm when Moriah abruptly came to a stop.

"I cannot move!" She anxiously tugged on a fold of her *stola*. It was snagged on something jutting from the building behind, imprisoning her.

Sparks from the inferno across the alley landed on the building's rooftop. Suddenly it burst into flame above Moriah's head. She screamed, her gaze shooting upward.

Aidan tore the fold from her hands. With a fierce tug, he ripped the material loose, freeing her, then pulled her forward and through the archway.

A deafening roar and crash, more horrible than the sound of a legion of advancing soldiers, shook the air behind them. In horror, the trio turned to watch as the tower imploded upon itself. Flaming wood crashed to the ground where they had stood, completely blocking the alley. Thousands of sparks flew through the air, setting nearby buildings on fire.

"My lady! Your *stola!*"

At Deborah's fearful words, Moriah looked down. Glowing dots of terrible orange covered the folds of white material.

Aidan dropped to his knees and slapped at the burning embers until only charred black holes remained.

"There's no way back," Deborah moaned, her hands covering her mouth as she looked in the direction they had come. "We are doomed!"

"No!" Aidan's voice was confident, bold. "The house I've told you about is this way. Come!"

He took hold of Moriah's wrist and raced down the street. Turning a corner, they darted past an overturned cart someone in haste had left in the narrow road. Several chickens ran out of the way, squawking amid the roar of the flames. Except for their presence, the area was deserted.

When the trio came to an intersecting street, they went left and ran down stone steps, then turned another corner to go through an archway, the hot breath of the fire beating down on their necks, threatening them with every step.

Aidan stopped abruptly, causing the women to almost barrel into him. Moriah looked past him to see.

In the midst of the blaze burning in all directions, a little girl, no more than six, knelt in the middle of the road not yet touched by the fire. A ragged tunic covered her shaking shoulders. Her small brown hands covered her eyes. Two still figures lay next to her on the ground.

Aidan rushed to the girl's side and knelt beside her. Taking hold of her shoulders, he tried to peer into her face. "What happened, Child?"

The girl quickly lifted her head. Her dirty features and watery eyes were full of terror mixed with despair. The child tried to wrench away, obviously frightened by their appearance.

"Be still. We mean you no harm," Aidan said.

"They killed them," the girl cried. "They killed Mama and Papa!"

Aidan released the child and turned over the crumpled body of the man. His blank stare reached the heavens. Bright light from nearby flames showed the dark blood soaking the front of his brown wool tunic. The sight of it sent the little girl into hysterical screams. They blended in with all the other screams sounding throughout Rome—the roar of the fires a terrible accompaniment to the cacophony.

Aidan closed the man's eyes with his fingers, and Deborah pulled the girl away from the grisly sight and close to her bosom. Moriah looked away from the dead man and at the child, whom Deborah tried so hard to console. Besides the fire, what other horrible sights had the little one seen this night? Who had done this to her parents and why?

Out of the corner of her eye, Moriah noticed a slight movement. She peered closely at the slim form of the child's mother. An arm twitched beneath the homespun cloak.

"Aidan!" Moriah moved to kneel beside the woman and touch the bony shoulder. "Aidan, she lives!"

He hastened Moriah's way, helping her turn the woman over to check her wounds. A terrible knot had formed on her bruised forehead, and a trickle of blood ran into her black hair. Her dusky face was pale, and her full lips were devoid of color.

Aidan inhaled sharply. "Naoni!"

Moriah turned from staring at the delicate features of the woman, her gaze going to Aidan's startled face. A twinge tugged at Moriah's heart, as a vague memory wafted through her brain like the black smoke drifting into the sky around them. Naoni?

She watched Aidan cradle the woman's head in his lap and push back damp tendrils of hair from her bloody face. He checked the wound, his eyes anxious, then put his ear to her mouth and exhaled in relief. "She breathes."

Naoni? Moriah thought. *Who is Naoni?* Then the cloudy memory took shape, and she knew. This was the woman of whom Aidan spoke that long-ago night in the garden. The woman who served in the house of Laurentius as a fellow slave and showed Aidan the way of Christianity. The woman whom Aidan said he would one day find.

Moriah averted her gaze, unable to watch the worry clouding his face as he looked at the lovely creature he held in his arms. Even bleeding and pale, she was beautiful.

Now Moriah understood why Aidan couldn't express his feelings the night she implored him to tell her he loved her. Now she understood the truth behind his reluctance to speak, though at the time she reasoned it was because he was a slave and she was a citizen. Now she knew.

Aidan loved this woman.

Moriah gripped her carved box until its corners dug into her soft palms. In the far recesses of her heart, she had nurtured the slim hope that somehow she and Aidan could be together one day. But her dreams were nothing more than ashes—so much like Rome, this proud city, was destined to become.

Hot tears filled Moriah's eyes, adding to the sting and burn from the smoke. A dark cloud crossed her mind. What reason was there to go on? Why should she not throw herself into one of the fires raging nearby and be done with it? If she and Rome did survive, her father would marry her to Servius, and such a fate surely would be worse than death. If she survived but Rome did not, then she forever would be faced with the knowledge that the man she loved cared for another. She could never be his. . .all was lost. . .lost. . .

"Moriah!"

Startled, she looked away from the hypnotic dancing flames and up at Aidan, barely taking note of the fact he called her by name. He stood, holding the unconscious Naoni in his arms. Deborah stood next to him, the child by her side. Both Aidan and Deborah had worried frowns on their faces.

"You were in a trance, my lady," Aidan said. "I called out to you, but you did not answer. We must hurry!" He motioned with his head toward an *insulae* in the distance. "The passage-way is through there. Come!"

Moriah rose, her heart swiftly pounding when she realized what a morbid trail her thoughts had taken. After so recently finding the one true God and feeling the warmth of His love and the sense of belonging, how could she consider such a terrible thing as to throw it all away? What madness had whispered to her mind in that dark moment?

She loved Aidan. Yet if she were destined to live without his love, without the joy of knowing him as her husband, to be denied the pleasure of lying in his arms. . .

Her eyes slid shut. She wiped away the tears trailing down her cheeks and lifted her chin.

Then she would find the strength to cope. She now had family to which she belonged, fellow Christians to see her through difficult times. That realization helped Moriah to stand taller, though her heart still bled inside.

⋟

The *insulae* at the end of the row stood dark and silent, a strange sight with the building that blazed beside it. The greedy talons of the fire had not yet touched its walls. Once inside, Aidan kicked at one of the closest doors at ground level with his sandaled foot. Hurriedly he pushed against the thick barrier with his shoulder to gain admittance.

The door swung open. The light from the flames behind them danced on the rock walls and dirt floor, casting a peculiar glow on the dark, unoccupied room. A crude table sat at the side of the dwelling, four stools, one overturned, around it.

"This way," Aidan said tersely, leading them to a wool blanket hanging from the ceiling, separating the room into two. He ducked behind the curtain. There, in the earthen floor, was an opening once concealed by the roughhewn cot that had been pushed aside.

"They have gone through the passage," Aidan said excitedly. "Gaius and his sons are builders—Jews converted to the Way. Two years ago, he felt the need to dig this entrance due to the constant persecution the Christians face. He told me about it. He is one of those who believes matters will grow worse instead of better," Aidan explained quickly. "We shall follow."

Moriah looked doubtfully into the small dark cavern. "There is no light. How will we see to find our way?"

Aidan laid the still form of Naoni on the cot. Grabbing an unlit torch, he disappeared outside. Soon he returned, a flame now jumping at the end of the thick piece of wood. Concern lit his eyes. "We must hurry!"

Moriah did not ask why. The distinct roar of the flames growing louder was answer enough. She accepted the torch Aidan handed her and watched as he again picked up Naoni, this time easily settling her over his shoulder.

"Careful, my lady. The steps are steep," he warned.

Moriah bent over at the waist and thrust the smoking torch into the dark hole of the cavern, trying to make out what lay beyond. Three narrow stone steps were revealed in the scant light of the flame. The rest were smothered in darkness.

Fighting back fear, she straightened, lifted the hem of her *stola* with one hand, and carefully stepped into the dark hole. Putting one hand to the earthen wall, she slowly proceeded down many rough steps until at last she reached bottom.

The first thing she noted was how cool the air was beneath the ground—a welcome sensation after practically being baked alive. But except for the flickering torchlight, she could not help but feel that a world of frightening blackness had swallowed her. The second thing she realized was that the ground was wet, though thankfully the water did not seep into her shoes.

Deborah and the child came down the stone steps and stood beside her. Aidan took up the rear, Naoni over his shoulder.

"You will have to lead the way, my lady," he said, his words hollow in the narrow passage. "I cannot carry the torch and Naoni safely. When we reach a place where the passage intersects with another, look upon the walls for the carving of a fish."

With torch held high, Moriah anxiously turned. Exercising caution, uncertain of what lay ahead, she crept along the dank corridor, too narrow for two people to walk abreast of one another. On each side, coarse volcanic rock rose, joining a short distance above their heads. The flame from the torch touched the ceiling of solid tufa rock.

Moriah felt as if the cold walls were pressing in on her. She was certain she would suffocate in such a confined space.

Prickles of fear stabbed her mind. What lay at the end of this dark tunnel? A way out—or another means of death?

After traveling for some time, they reached an intersecting gallery wider than the passage they were in. Moriah lifted the torch to the left side of the tufa wall. Nothing. She brought it to the right side. There, barely discernable, someone had carved a line drawing of a fish into the stone.

"This way," she said, her voice trembling in the emptiness.

They moved into a wide corridor. Rectangular openings cut from the tufa rock rose horizontally, one on top of the other, to the high ceiling. Moriah knew that beyond the marble slabs covering those openings rested the departed. A shiver that had nothing to do with the bone-chilling cold shook her body. To be this close to death unnerved her, and she wished they were far from this place.

"We have reached the catacombs," Aidan said in relief. "Which means we are outside the city walls."

The many twists and turns seemed endless, a labyrinth of passages and galleries leading to more galleries. At times they walked up a short series of steps; at other times they descended. The stale air was close, and Moriah gulped each breath, wondering how she could breathe at all. Yet compared to the heat of the fires that raged far above their heads and the acrid, suffocating smoke that accompanied the destructive flames, the discomfort was relatively minor.

Upon reaching an imposing structure that Aidan informed her was an *arcosolium,* the grave of a wealthy man, Moriah held her torch above the stone and made out the inscription of a seven-branched candlestick, one of many she had seen in the passages.

"A sign of the Jew," Deborah whispered in Moriah's ear, the first time she had spoken since going beneath ground. "This is where my people lay their dead to rest."

Moriah held back a shiver and walked farther. Ahead, she discerned the sound of faint weeping and murmuring voices.

"We are nearing the others," Aidan said. "When we reach

them, it will be easier to breathe because of the *luminaria*. The holes are cut into the ceiling of rock to bring fresh air into the chamber," he explained, as though anticipating Moriah's next question. "With the *luminaria,* Gaius's plans to live underground for a short time could be possible."

Moriah vaguely listened to Aidan's words, realizing he said them to pacify her fear rather than to relay information. Yet one thought niggled at her mind. She remembered his earlier comments about persecution. She, too, was now a Christian. Would she face persecution or worse—a fate such as her parents had confronted? Would her newfound faith be tested so soon?

Moriah did not feel especially brave and wondered how she would fare should such circumstances come her way. Brushing aside the chilling thought, she ducked her head under the low ceiling of the opening and led the way into the dimly lit underground room.

≈

"And so my beloved brothers and sisters, we must remember what Paul wrote in his letters and what he spoke when last he walked among us." The grizzled elder continued to reassure the small gathering of frightened people who sat on the stone floor and stood along the tufa walls. A few injured lay near their loved ones. "We must be strong, knowing that our Lord is the rock on which we stand. He will protect us, come what may."

Several torches lined the walls, casting their glow over the dim chamber. Moriah sat with her back against a wall, Deborah next to her. The child—who had told them her name was Laniah—rested with her head in Deborah's lap. Beside her, Naoni still lay unconscious on the ground.

"My lady," Aidan whispered as he moved to the other side of Moriah and crouched low. "Are you well?"

Troubled, Moriah looked at him. This was the first time he had addressed her since they joined this small band of Christians, mostly made up of converted Jews.

"Aidan, what is to become of us?"

Yellow light from a nearby torch flickered across his solemn features, and his mouth tightened. "If Rome survives, I have been instructed by Clophelius to return you to the house."

She shook her head. "No, I do not mean what is to become of me. I mean to us." She motioned with her hand to include the twelve other people in the cavelike room. "To all of us."

Aidan hesitated. "You need not fear, my lady. We are safe from the fire and will soon be able to leave this place."

She shook her head. "Again, you misunderstand. I speak of the persecutions you mentioned earlier. For, you see, I, too, am a Christian."

Something sparked in his eyes. Something that made Moriah's heart beat a little faster and interfered with her breathing as he continued to stare.

"You have become one of us?" he asked.

"Yes. That is why I sought you in the garden tonight. . . yesterday. . .whatever day it was. That moment seems lost, as though it took place in another time. Yet for all I am aware, it could have been only hours since I spoke of jasmine and such trivial matters." She shook her head at her foolishness and managed a tight smile. "I wished to tell you then, but I was nervous—"

A throaty groan interrupted her. Moriah turned to see Naoni slowly moving her head from side to side, obviously in a great deal of pain.

"Mama!" Laniah crawled away from Deborah's lap. "Mama, please wake up!"

Aidan also moved toward the prone woman. Moriah watched Naoni's eyelids flutter open, revealing light brown eyes glazed with confusion. Naoni looked at the child by her side, and relief crossed her face. Her gaze flicked to the man hovering above her, and her eyes widened.

"Aidan?" Her voice was husky. "Is it truly you?" She moved to sit up. With another groan, she sank back to the stone floor, putting a hand to her head.

"Praise be to God that you are alive," Aidan said, his voice choked with emotion. "We came upon you and your child in the street—" He broke off, his expression uneasy.

Naoni's eyes darkened. "Linus? My husband, where is he?"

Aidan took her hand, his gaze lowering to the slim brown fingers. "I am sorry, Naoni. He is dead."

The woman released a shaky breath and closed her eyes. After a moment she spoke. "The soldiers stopped us, Aidan."

"Stopped you? From what?"

"Linus tried to quench the fire and almost succeeded in doing so to the building next to ours. But a soldier suddenly came from nowhere and struck him, then threw more fuel onto the flames. Linus tried to save our *insulae* when it also caught fire—" Tears choked her words. "And another soldier ran him through with his sword. I screamed and rushed toward them, but I remember nothing after that." Her gaze went to her small daughter, who listened, her face solemn. "Oh, Aidan," Naoni murmured softly. "What shall Laniah and I do? We have nothing left."

Aidan took the distraught woman in his arms and tried to comfort her. Naoni clutched him as though he were her anchor.

Moriah turned away, her heart bleeding with fresh pain. The thought stabbed her mind that now there was nothing to prevent the two from a future together. Naoni no longer had a husband, and Aidan had found his love. The woman would need someone to take care of her and her daughter. If Clophelius survived the fire and allowed Aidan to take a bride, Moriah was sure he would choose Naoni.

Abruptly the woman's story fully penetrated Moriah's weary mind, producing a fear to rival anything she had been through that night. Her eyes widened.

Naoni had said soldiers worked to feed the fire rather than to stop it. What if the words Clophelius had spoken were true? Was Nero the mastermind behind this evil deed? And if it were so, what would it mean to Rome? To its people?

A serpent of deep foreboding twined itself around Moriah's heart, squeezing until she could scarcely breathe. She did not know from where the thought originated, but she knew something more terrible than the fire was soon to come their way.

eleven

Arms crossed, Aidan stood with his back against the rock wall near the entrance to one of many small chambers underground and listened while Gaius tried to convince two men in their group of his plan. It had been days since the fires started, though no one knew how many. A man and his wife had left for the city some time earlier but soon returned, shaken, with news that the fires were still raging and the destruction was vast. There was nowhere else to go, so the gathering remained.

"Consider this," Gaius said, his gaze encompassing each of the six men in the room. "Daily our numbers increase, as does Rome's hatred for our kind. You have seen what one tunnel can do. If we had others spread throughout the city with hidden entrances—"

"Hidden entrances?" Urbanus, a baker, scoffed. "You speak of such bizarre ideas yet seem to have forgotten that we must rebuild our homes. Besides, why should we hide? I am not convinced we are in any lasting danger."

"Are you blind?" Gaius's son Matthias asked. "Did you not see what they did to Timothy and Pergus two weeks past? They beat them severely."

"A handful of misguided Jews. . ."

"Which is what we were before we converted to the Faith," Junias, the elder, quietly reminded.

"Lately it is not only the Jews who rise up against us," Gaius's eldest son, Philip, inserted. "It seems everyone in Rome has turned against the Christians." The men sobered, and Philip looked Aidan's way. "What do you think, Aidan? We have not yet heard from you."

Aidan somberly regarded each man before speaking. "Gaius's words have merit. Yet to where would such tunnels

152

lead? Here?" He motioned to the cavelike walls surrounding them and shook his head. "You forget, my friends, these are Jewish catacombs. We would not be safe in such a place."

"Why do we not build our own?" Philip asked.

"And from where would the funding come? Nero?" Urbanus's reply was mocking. "There is a city to rebuild."

"Then what is the answer?" Philip insisted. "You heard Naoni's story. We cannot trust those who serve the empire. The soldiers burned our homes."

"True, but they did not burn only the homes of the Christians."

"And that's supposed to give me comfort?" Philip's reply was incredulous.

"Aidan." Deborah's brusque voice interrupted them as she came to the entrance of the chamber. "I would have a word with you."

"Is Naoni worse?" Philip half rose from the ground, concern in his dark eyes.

"No, she is only sleeping," Deborah said more softly.

Aidan noted the relief sweep across the young man's features. He flushed red when he noticed Aidan's stare and looked away. Aidan smiled. Naoni and her child would be well cared for. Philip was a good man and obviously cared for Naoni. Though Philip was a few years younger than the woman, Aidan felt certain that in due time Gaius would give his consent to the match.

"Aidan."

He turned to Deborah. She regarded him gravely. "I would speak with you. Now. Before my lady awakens."

Aidan nodded, and they moved down a passage and into another alcove. They had no more than set foot inside the small chamber when Deborah swiftly turned. "I warned you weeks ago not to speak to Moriah."

"That hardly has been possible since Clophelius made me her bodyguard."

She impatiently flicked her hand upward at his reply. "You know to what I refer, Aidan. Do not play the fool. You spoke to her of your faith, and now she has accepted this Christianity and is in danger."

A ray of joy shone through Aidan's heavy heart at the reminder. Since Moriah revealed news of her conversion, he and she had spoken of it a few times but on each occasion were interrupted by someone needing counsel or aid. Several times Aidan preached words of encouragement to one or more members of their group and found himself in the position of discipling them. The experience had been a rewarding one, though Moriah's maidservant had left the chamber each time.

"And what would you have me say, Deborah?" he asked soberly. "That I'm sorrowed to learn my lady has found the road to everlasting life and has followed in the footsteps of her father and mother?"

"Who are now dead because of it," Deborah returned bitterly. "Is that the fate you also wish for Moriah?"

"Of course not. Yet neither do I wish for her to live in eternal damnation, which will happen to those who do not accept Jesus as their Lord. I have prayed for her to find the truth for years." At her scowl, he softened his demeanor. "Can you honestly say, Deborah, that her mother, whom you served, would not be overjoyed to learn that Moriah has become a follower of the Way? If Moriah's mother were alive, do you hesitate to think that she would not have raised her daughter in the Faith?"

His quiet words had a powerful impact on the tiny woman. What looked like shame crossed her face, and deep furrows lined her brow. Her eyes shone with confusion before she turned and left him.

Remorse filled Aidan at his harsh dealing with her. She was fighting the Truth, and it was not until that moment that he realized she feared it. He would add her to his prayers.

As Aidan moved toward the main chamber, his heart beat swiftly at the prospect of what lay ahead. He also had news. News for Moriah that he had not yet shared. The thought of what it could mean to them caused his mouth to go dry, and he quickened his steps in search of her.

❧

"My lady, may I speak with you?"

Moriah started and looked away from the gallery wall, up at Aidan's solemn countenance. "Of course."

She had felt the need to separate herself from the others for a time, to sit and rest and think about the future—if there was a future. Since the night they'd come here, she'd helped Deborah tend the five wounded in their group. Including Moriah, there were four women, one of them elderly, seven men, and three children. Moriah was amazed at the satisfaction she gained from serving others instead of being served. But the almost constant work, foreign to her, made her weary in both mind and body.

Aidan knelt beside her and offered a dry crust torn from one of the loaves. "You must eat. The sack of bread Urbanus brought from his bakery when he fled will last for a time. And we have Mathias's wineskin of water. We shall not starve or thirst," he added. "The fires cannot go on much longer."

Moriah looked at the unappetizing morsel in his hand. She knew she should eat, but her stomach rebelled at the thought. "No, Aidan. I cannot."

His eyes grew concerned. "At least take some water," he suggested, holding a small dipper full of the life-giving liquid toward her.

Moriah nodded, and Aidan held the wooden cup to her lips. Though the liquid was not as cool as it could be, it felt good to her throat, still raw from the smoke she had inhaled. Wearily, she settled back against the wall. "Is Naoni faring well?"

"As well as can be expected."

Moriah lowered her gaze to Aidan's soot-streaked tunic. "She is very lovely—in both form and spirit. I can see why you love her."

Moriah heard him gasp but did not look up. She didn't want to see the effect of her words softening his face or the light that must surely be in his eyes at the mention of Naoni. She forced herself to speak. "In the time I have come to know her,

I've found Naoni to be a remarkable woman. You spoke rightly when first you mentioned her that long-ago night in the garden. She is without resentment against those who have done her harm. Much like my parents were, I expect."

"My lady, I have something I must tell you. Something I've wanted to share before now, but there never seemed an opportune moment."

Curious, she lifted her head. A strange light did glow in his eyes, but Moriah was uncertain if it was due to love. "Yes, Aidan?" she whispered, wondering if he would now admit his feelings for Naoni.

"I am no longer a slave."

Moriah stared. Her lifeblood felt as though it were draining away through the cold rock floor, causing her to feel faint. She was glad she was sitting down.

"No longer a slave?" she repeated numbly.

"Clophelius granted me my freedom before we left the house. I shared the gospel message with him, and though he was not pleased to learn of my Christianity, he chose to set me free. Indeed, he told me he planned to do so all along, but my words further persuaded him."

"Free," she repeated, her voice a mere wisp of sound.

The thought that now she would never see him again slammed across her mind. Yet perhaps this was better. If Aidan returned to Rome a slave, assuming the house still stood, it would have been torture for Moriah to see him and Naoni together as man and wife—and as the years passed, to see the children that resulted from their union.

"I am happy for you, Aidan," she said, trying to instill a measure of joy into her words. Knowing she had failed miserably and uncertain what else there was to say, she lowered her gaze to the front of his tunic.

In the main chamber, someone began to sing a hymn for God's deliverance and protection, as many had done throughout the long vigil. Other voices joined in, breaking the heavy quiet that suddenly descended between the two.

Aidan moved his hand to cover hers. Moriah thought her heart would cease beating. Her head snapped up in surprise.

"I do not love Naoni," he said, so softly she almost could not hear him. His gaze was mesmerizing. "I love you."

To her amazement, Aidan leaned closer and brushed his lips over hers in a gentle kiss.

A thousand cymbals crashed inside her brain. Warmth touched the core of her being, spreading throughout her veins like liquid fire. She lifted her hands to clutch his tunic and bring him closer. His arms went around her, and he deepened the kiss.

Moriah exulted, never wanting the moment to end. Here there were no soldiers to prompt Aidan into doing such a thing. Nor had she needed to beg him to hold her. Aidan kissed her because he desired it, because he loved her, and that knowledge filled Moriah with such happiness she could scarcely contain it.

The singing abruptly came to a halt, but she thought nothing of it. When one set of hollow footsteps echoed down the passageway near the main entrance and toward them, she barely was aware of the small disturbance and wished whoever it was would leave them be.

Suddenly Aidan was hauled from her. The ominous ring of a sword being pulled from its sheath filled the still air. Moriah blinked, disoriented. She looked in horror to Aidan sprawled on the ground, the point of a gleaming sword positioned at the hollow of his throat—then up to the Roman soldier who stood in a lunge and wielded the deadly weapon.

"Paulus," she breathed in disbelief.

He ignored her. His eyes burned with hatred, and a pulse throbbed in his cheek. "Get up, scum!" he ordered Aidan. "And say a prayer to your God before you die!"

"Paulus—no!" Moriah shot up from the ground and moved toward Aidan. Spinning around to face Paulus, she placed herself between the angry soldier and the man she loved and wrapped both hands around Paulus's sword arm. It was as hard and immovable as iron. She was dizzy from lack of food, but determination surged hot in her veins, giving her strength. "He has done no wrong."

"I saw him, Moriah," Paulus gritted. "I saw him dare to kiss you."

Underneath her hands, his arm moved, and Aidan gasped. Alarmed, Moriah turned to look. A trickle of blood appeared on Aidan's neck near the hollow of his throat.

"No!" Moriah dug her nails into Paulus's arm, trying to push it away. "He has done no wrong. Do not harm him! Please, Paulus. Listen to me!"

Paulus turned to fully look at Moriah for the first time. His jaw grew hard as he clenched his teeth. "What enchantment have these Christians placed on you, Moriah? What sorcery have they practiced to cloud your mind to the truth?"

"No sorcery, Paulus," she replied, her voice wavering. "And I know the truth for the first time in my life. Please, sheathe your sword."

He studied her awhile longer, then straightened and slowly did as she requested, watching with narrowed eyes as Aidan stood to his feet. "I have come to take you back to the house, Moriah," he said, his voice hard. "It was no easy task finding you. Only from a chance conversation I overheard this morning between two of many flocked outside the gates did I learn that some sought the catacombs for refuge—and in their company was a patrician's daughter, her bodyguard, and her maid."

"The house still stands?" Moriah's words were hopeful. "And Clophelius—he is well?"

Paulus gave a curt nod, his gaze never leaving Aidan. "When Nero learned the Palatine was in danger, we returned, but by that time the scope of the fires was much too vast to stop. Rome is a wasteland of smoking ruins. Only four of the districts escaped destruction. Three regions are leveled, including the Palatine, and seven are seriously damaged. The house stands, though not unharmed. The fire touched it as well."

"And Clophelius?" Moriah's words were hoarse.

"Before the fires overtook the Caelian Hill, Senator Valerius came for my uncle and insisted he seek shelter. Against his will, he was carried to safety."

"I am relieved to hear it," Moriah murmured. "Is the fire completely extinguished?"

"After five days, it was put out, but a second fire started in another part of the city. Rome burned for nine days."

"Nine days," Moriah breathed in shock.

Paulus felt his tense expression relax as he looked at her. "I have spoken with Uncle Clophelius in great depth. You need not marry Servius Antonus. Uncle has agreed to a match between us when my commission in the army is finished this year."

Moriah blinked, slowly shaking her head. "I cannot marry you, Paulus. I love another."

His gaze whipped to Aidan. "He is but a slave, Moriah! And you are the daughter of a patrician. There can be no future for you with such a man."

"He has been freed." Moriah looked at Aidan, her expression tender. "And he is the man I choose."

Paulus inhaled sharply, his breath whistling through his teeth. "By all that is sacred, he *has* placed an enchantment on you! He and these other Christians. But Nero will soon deal with their kind."

"What do you mean?" Moriah swiftly returned her attention to Paulus.

"I have heard that Nero may need a scapegoat, someone on whom to place blame for the fire. I have also heard he has found a possible solution to the problem." Paulus looked to the group of people curiously huddled together at the entrance, his gesture making it clear to all about whom he spoke.

"Nero burned Rome?" Moriah asked in a tight voice.

"There have been rumors circulating." Paulus shrugged. "I do not know. But the people are angry and crying for justice to be served. As a soldier, loyal to the empire, it is my duty to honor that wish." His hand tightened on the hilt of his sword. "Nero would be pleased if I was to bring him his first victims," he threatened, eyeing the others. "And I will, Moriah. Unless you come with me."

She straightened to her full height. "I cannot come with you. And if you take these people to Nero, then you must take me, as well. For I am one of them now."

Paulus's eyes widened. "Moriah, no. He is not worth this! Do not lie to save his skin."

"I do not lie," she said quietly. "I am a Christian."

At his look of shocked horror, she took a step toward him and continued. "You once told me that you did not believe the Christian religion engaged in the horrible practices rumor has whispered. Well, Paulus, you were right."

She lifted her hands in supplication, her eyes, the tone of her voice, pleading with him to understand. "You knew my father—my true father—and admired him these many years, or so you told me. Do you sincerely believe he would belong to a sect that would hurt others or set fire to an entire city and destroy its people?"

At his continued silence, she went on, and suddenly it was as though someone else spoke through her. "Whether Nero was responsible for the horror I and thousands of others suffered, I do not know. But I do know this. A madman was responsible for those fires. Fires that consumed everything in their paths, leaving nothing except a trail of destruction in their wake. But Jesus the Christ, the Son of the Most High God whom I've accepted, is a God of love and mercy."

She lifted her lips in a small smile. "I have experienced the depth of His love, Paulus. It's like a flame burning within, warming my heart and breathing life into my soul. Those of us who are His followers have known the wonder of His love burning within our breasts. It changes a person, Paulus. It truly does."

He only stared, his mouth slack with disbelief.

"The fire that ravaged Rome brought nothing but pain and destruction and was the result of a depraved mind," she emphasized solemnly. "But the fire that comes from the Lord brings healing and restoration. It yields nothing but His love."

Paulus spoke, his voice tight with contained emotion. "And what about us, Moriah? What about my love for you?"

"Remember the day in the garden after we left the circus?" she asked quietly, reminding him of their kiss and the discomfort it evoked. "I have loved you, Paulus, as a dear cousin. And though now I know you are not my cousin, I will continue to care for you, as I always have, until death overtakes me." Her forehead creased—the only sign of apprehension on her features. "Whether that day comes sooner than expected is your decision. But these people are my family. And this is where I belong."

Defeat caused Paulus's shoulders to slump, and he shook his head. "Do you truly believe I could take your life, Moriah?" His gaze flicked over the group of anxious Christians, then back to her. "I do not understand your God, but I know you. You would not pledge your loyalty to someone you did not fully trust. You are more clever than that." He swallowed hard. "Neither you nor your friends shall see harm by my hand. I vow this to you."

The relief in the chamber was palpable, though no one spoke. Paulus looked at the others, then back to Moriah.

"But a word of warning," he added. "Both Nero and Poppaea are aware of you and your true parentage. In Antium, I heard Nero speak of it to Tigellinus, seeking his advice. The prefect has told him of your rare beauty, and Nero showed interest in bringing you to the palace, though he wasn't pleased to hear who your true father was. Since it is no longer possible for you to claim ignorance to Christianity, should Nero summon you to pledge your allegiance to him and the empire and perhaps even to renounce any fealty to this Christ. . ." An urgency filled his voice. "You must leave Rome with all haste. You are no longer safe here. Do you understand, Moriah?"

A dazed expression covered her face, but she nodded.

His gaze slowly traveled over her features once more, then his jaw tightened, and he turned to go. Before he could walk away, Moriah put her hand to his arm.

"Paulus, wait." She looked toward Deborah and saw Laniah standing close by. "Laniah, please bring me my box."

The child nodded and hurried away. Soon she returned, her terrified gaze fastened on Paulus as she handed Moriah the requested item. The child darted back to Deborah, whose arms went around the girl. Moriah dug something from within the silver and ivory container and placed it in Paulus's hand. Puzzled, he looked down at the statuette of a jade cat.

"I found it at the market—for your birthday. It reminded me of Claudius," she explained, tears clouding her eyes. "I want you to have it, Paulus—to remember me."

"Little dove, I could never forget you."

She went to him and hugged him. Paulus tightened his arms around her, and she knew he understood they would never see each other again.

twelve

"My lady, you are certain of this?"

Moriah looked into Deborah's troubled eyes, her heart at peace. "I am certain. I love him, Deborah."

The woman's brow creased, though she gave a short nod. "I only wish for your happiness. If your mother were here, she would want the same." She paused and looked away. "I've decided to stay in Rome. Naoni has asked this of me, and Laniah needs me. You no longer do. In truth, I never approved of Aidan, but he will take care of you. He has proven himself worthy in that regard."

Moriah's first instinct was to plead with Deborah to change her mind, but she realized her maidservant was right. Deborah had grown attached to the child Laniah, who had seemed to withdraw into a private world and had barely spoken since Paulus left the catacombs a short time ago. Still, Moriah had not realized her decision would cause her to lose Deborah's companionship. Perhaps such a thing was best. Deborah was in no danger and had nothing to fear by staying in Rome. Moriah's future was uncertain. Deborah's decision was the right one.

She put her arms around the woman and kissed her cheek. "I shall dearly miss you, my friend. What will I do without you?"

Deborah returned her affection, and Moriah felt the woman's tears against her face. "Please, Deborah," Moriah felt the urge to say. "Listen to the words of Naoni. Do not allow fear to keep you from the Truth. Will you do this for me?"

Deborah pulled away, her expression uncertain, but she nodded. "Your bridegroom awaits, my lady. I wish you were able to wear the traditional orange veil, but I'm certain Aidan will not care that you are without it. At least I managed to remove the soot from your skin, and your face is glowing as brightly as the moon." The smile she offered was feeble at best, and Moriah squeezed her hand.

Together they walked into another chamber lit with torch-light. Moriah joined Aidan, whose eyes held adoration for her, and they turned to stand before Junias. The others gathered round. One of the women sniffled.

The elder regarded them with a paternal smile. "Aidan, I look upon you as a son and am pleased with your choice of a bride. I have long prayed for this day, and I ask the Lord Jesus to watch over this joyful occasion and guide me in the words to speak. For where two or three are gathered in His name, there He is also."

"Let it be so," Aidan whispered.

"Cherish this woman you have chosen, Aidan. Sustain and protect her always. Love her as Christ loves the Church and gave Himself up for it, even to the point of death. So must you be willing to sacrifice your life for her. As you love your own body, love her, in all circumstances."

"I will." Aidan's reply came without hesitation.

Junias looked at Moriah. "My lady, be subject to this man in all things, as to the Lord. Give him the honor he deserves. Stand beside him and be his helpmate. Revere him as your husband and esteem him highly."

"I shall do so." Moriah's heart felt as if it would take flight, as fast as it beat within her breast.

From somewhere Junias produced a long cord. He took Aidan's hand and placed it over Moriah's, then loosely bound them together with the cord. "Be subject one to another, beloved, for we are all one in Christ Jesus. There is neither male nor female, slave nor free, Gentile nor Jew, but all are one in Him. Remember Christ in all you do. Do not forget that each of you has been released from the shackles of bondage and are called out to live holy lives, free from all unrighteousness."

"We will live for Him," Aidan said, and Moriah echoed his words.

Junias motioned them both to kneel and placed his hands

on their foreheads. He spoke a heartfelt blessing over their union, praying for God's protection, guidance, and wisdom in all things. When he finished, his eyes glowed with happiness.

"May our Lord God smile upon you and bless your union with many children. I sense in my spirit that the Lord has important plans for you. Do not fear the future, beloved, but trust in God. Adversity will come, but *El Elyon,* the Most High God, will watch over you and be your rear guard. Confidently rely on Him."

Junias unbound the cord from their hands and stepped back, indicating an end to the ceremony. His smile was wide. "Go in peace, my children, together as man and wife."

A cheer went up for the bridal couple. Aidan rose to his feet, pulling Moriah up with him, and Philip clapped him on the shoulder in enthusiastic congratulations. The others offered their blessings, as well. In normal circumstances, feasting and dancing would follow. Still, despite the somber conditions, the brief wedding had brought a smile to everyone's face.

Later, the others slipped into the main chamber to give the couple some privacy. Moriah turned to the man who was now her husband. With infinite gentleness, Aidan cradled her face, his fingers against her neck as he brushed his thumbs over her jaw. Moriah could only stare; her heart was so full of love for him, so full of awe that her dream at last had been realized.

"My lady. . ." His words were hoarse with emotion.

Moriah smiled tenderly, her own throat clogged with happy tears. "What happened to 'Moriah'?"

He let out a soft chuckle. "After nine years of addressing you as 'my lady,' it may be difficult to assume the habit of calling you by your given name. But I shall try."

"Please do."

A grin lifted the corners of his mouth, and he tilted her face upward. "Moriah."

Tingles raced down her spine. Warmth flooded her from head to toe at the husky way he spoke her name and the gentle kiss he bestowed on her lips.

"Never call me anything else," she murmured when he lifted his head.

Aidan's hands moved to her shoulders. "Not 'Beloved' or 'Dear Wife'?" he asked with another smile.

"In that case, I shall make an exception."

The torchlight flashed on the slave bracelet still covering his upper arm. Moriah's hands went to it, and she worked to get the jammed catch to unfasten, then threw the despised token to the stone floor with a loud *ching*.

"No regrets?" His mood turned serious.

Moriah lifted one hand to cradle the side of his strong face. Immediately he covered her hand with his, trapping it.

"Never," she whispered. "I have loved you from the moment I understood what it meant to be a woman, Aidan. If it were possible, I would have married you then. I need, or want, nothing more than you and God in my life. And one day our child to hold in my arms."

His eyes shone with tears, and his hands lowered to her waist, drawing her close. "Moriah, my beloved," he whispered before his lips met hers in a passionate kiss, promising much and sending her head into a whirl.

Another flame began to burn deep within, different from the fire of the Lord's about which she had so recently told Paulus, but containing its own all-consuming love. The love she would share with this man who was now her husband.

Moriah threaded her fingers through Aidan's hair, and he drew her closer still.

❧

"My lady," the child Hannah said from nearby, in what seemed to Aidan an extremely short time later. The girl masked a giggle. "The elder says that the hour has come for you to depart. Darkness has fallen."

Reluctantly Aidan and Moriah broke their embrace. They stared into one another's eyes for one more stolen moment before turning their heads to look at the young girl who stood at the entrance.

"Thank you, Hannah. Tell Junias we shall come soon," Aidan said, giving her a smile.

Hannah hurried away, and Moriah looked back at Aidan. "Now that the time has arrived, I am frightened."

He took her hand and brought her fingertips to his lips. "You need not fear, Moriah. I have papers of freedom underneath my tunic, and you have your jewels with which to secure passage on a ship or obtain other means of transportation if need be. After all that has happened in Rome, no one will question your desire to leave."

"But where will we go?"

"I care not, as long as we are far from this city," Aidan said adamantly. The idea of Moriah in danger sent icy prickles of fear down his back. When she had confronted Paulus earlier and spoken up for Aidan and the others, she had reminded him of an avenging angel, fearless and bold, filling him with awe. She was more courageous than she realized, but he could not allow her to consider staying.

She stepped forward and nestled her head against his chest, putting her arms around his waist. Powerful sensations of love and protection soared through Aidan, and he lifted his hands to her back. He could scarcely believe that she was truly his, that God had blessed him so mightily by giving him the desire of his heart.

"I am thankful I shall always have you to watch over me," she murmured and again sought his gaze. "But what of the others, Aidan? What if the words Paulus spoke were true? Naoni and little Laniah and Philip and Junias and the others—could they be in danger? I feel guilty leaving them, though I am uncertain how I could help if we did stay."

Aidan stiffened and tightened his hold around her. "Your time in Rome has ended, Beloved. For us to even consider living in a different part of the city—whatever is left of the city—would be dangerous. Your beauty is extraordinary. It reached the eyes of those on the senate and others, besides."

She blushed, but he shook his head.

"Though I consider myself a fortunate man, I do not speak the words to flatter but rather to caution. With a countenance and form such as yours, you would be unable to hide yourself for long. Caesar has eyes and ears everywhere and a jealous empress besides. A Roman did not hesitate to turn your father in. Do you think you would be spared when an honored tribune was not? As to our friends. . ." He sighed and again cradled her head to his chest, intertwining his fingers into her thick hair. "I do not know what will happen. I cannot predict the future. All we can do is trust them to God's protection. We can do no more."

She sniffed, and Aidan pulled back. His thumb brushed over her cheek to wipe away a tear. "We must not be anxious for anything, Moriah. We need only have faith and trust in God."

"Yes, my husband. I only wish I had your deep faith."

He gave her a tender smile. "It will come in time."

"Aidan! Moriah! Make haste!"

Junias's deep bass echoed down the narrow passage and into the small chamber. Hearing the urgency in his voice, the two kissed once more, then broke apart.

Moriah's eyes glistened, but she gave him a shaky smile. "You are right, Aidan. We will trust the Lord to guide us."

"And He will." Unable to resist, he bent one final time to kiss his courageous bride before grabbing the torch from the tufa wall.

epilogue

Moriah basked in the warm ray of sunshine as she sat beside a narrow stream. She lifted her gaze to the majestic trees, so deeply green they appeared almost black. Slivers of pale sunlight pushed their way through leafy boughs. Pungent aromas of freshly watered earth and vegetation tantalized her nostrils. Peculiar birdcalls shattered the air, now familiar to Moriah after almost two years in this remote part of the world, where the empire had not invaded.

Thinking of the city of her birth, she gazed at the glimpse of blue heavens and said a prayer for those in Rome, wishing she knew what had become of them. Each morning she and Aidan held hands and prayed, entrusting their loved ones to God's care. It was all they could do, but as Aidan often told her, prayer was powerful. And God had blessed her mightily.

A movement next to Moriah caught her eye. Shaking her head in exasperation and laughing, she reached over and grabbed up one of her blessings before he could crawl into the stream sparkling in the light of the sun.

"No, no, Enud," she cooed, holding him at eye-level.

"Nuh-o, E-ed." His dark blue eyes crinkled at the corners as he tried to imitate her words. He clutched a handful of his fair-colored ringlets, then moved his hand to grab a thick lock of her dark hair flowing free past her waist.

Children's shouts from the nearby village brought his head around. Moriah also looked toward the commotion and watched the fair-headed children at play.

After escaping Rome, she and Aidan had traveled north for weeks, both by land and sea, until they reached this remote forest untouched by civilization. Though at first they were regarded with suspicion and contempt, they trusted that God's eternal flame of love burning within them would span the breach. Aidan built a thatched hut close to the village, but far enough away so as not to incur the people's wrath. Two months after their arrival, Moriah almost died when her food was laced with a deadly herb. After that, Aidan was determined to take his wife and go elsewhere.

On the night before they were to leave, Moriah again heard heavenly voices lifted in song, seeming to come from the direction of the village—but these voices were nothing like the villagers' chants. Moriah told Aidan about it, convinced God wanted them to stay. He regarded her in wonder, as he had when she first told him about her initial experience on the night of her conversion, but he took it as a sign to pray for guidance. Aidan, too, was convicted that God wanted them to remain.

Only one week passed before Aidan came close to losing his life to save a young boy from a wild boar. Afterward, some of the villagers slowly came to accept Aidan and Moriah. Once the language barrier was breached, they listened while Aidan powerfully told of the one true God who sacrificed His Son to save all people. Still, they didn't believe. Yet, after seeing evidence of God's love displayed through Aidan and Moriah in countless ways, several questioned. None had turned from their pagan roots, but Moriah sensed a difference in two of the young women when she spoke to them of Jesus and felt the time was near for their salvation. The thought filled her with joy.

"This was my destiny, was it not, Lord?" she whispered. "To be a helpmate to Aidan and to aid him in bringing the gospel to a people who never heard of You." They still had their trials and sorrows, but God carried them through each one, and Moriah's faith grew stronger with each situation.

The crunch of footsteps brought her head around. She smiled at Aidan, who sank to the ground beside her for a well-deserved rest. Enud's plump hands swung out to his father. Aidan reached for the boy and rubbed his bearded face on the child's bare tummy. Enud squealed gleefully.

Moriah regarded the two in mock frustration. "You surely

will spoil him, Aidan, as you have me." She tried to say the words sternly, though she couldn't keep from smiling.

His brows winged upward. "Spoil him, my lady?" he teased while reaching for her with his other arm and drawing her down to lie beside him on the mossy earth.

Moriah laughingly protested but chose to snuggle closer, resting her head on his shoulder. With his father's large hand protectively on his back, Enud happily claimed his spot sprawled on Aidan's glistening chest and slapped the bronzed skin with one baby palm. Aidan chuckled, and Enud squealed at the reverberations this made.

"If loving can spoil him—or you—I can think of a worse fate to be had." A gleam lit the deep blue of Aidan's eyes as he took his focus off their son and turned his head her way. "Would you honestly have me cease loving either of you as strongly as I do, Moriah?" His hand moved to her bulging belly and slowly rubbed a circle on the soft hide of her dress. "Or the child you now carry? It is not much, but love is all I have to offer."

Though his words were light, there was a hint of seriousness to them, as though he truly sought her feelings on the matter.

Moriah sensed he sometimes feared that she yearned for her former life of wealth in place of the meager existence they now shared. In the beginning, it had been difficult to grow accustomed to this vastly different mode of living without any of the luxuries she once took for granted. To serve rather than be served. Yet, with Aidan's patient help, Moriah had learned what she needed to know to survive in such a world. And she would not trade her life with Aidan and being the mother of his children for all the gold in Rome.

"Your love is all I desire, my husband," she breathed, laying her hand against his side. "Never think otherwise."

She leaned up on one hand and bent over, lowering her face to his. With her kiss, she showed him just how much she treasured the priceless gift of his love and returned that same gift. Gladness filled her heart, and Moriah was grateful she belonged—to Aidan, to her children, and to God.

SEATTLE

S hepherd of Love Hospital stands as a beacon of hope in Seattle, Washington. Its Christian staff members work with each other—and with God—to care for the sick and injured. But sometimes they find their own lives in need of a healing touch.

Can those who heal find healing for their own souls? How will the Shepherd for whom their hospital is named reveal the love each one longs for?

Contemporary, paperback, 480 pages, 5 ³⁄₁₆" x 8"

A Letter To Our Readers

Dear Reader:

In order that we might better contribute to your reading enjoyment, we would appreciate your taking a few minutes to respond to the following questions. We welcome your comments and read each form and letter we receive. When completed, please return to the following:

Fiction Editor
Heartsong Presents
PO Box 719
Uhrichsville, Ohio 44683

1. Did you enjoy reading *The Flame Within* by Pamela Griffin?
   ❑ Very much! I would like to see more books by this author!
   ❑ Moderately. I would have enjoyed it more if

   _____

   _____

   _____

2. Are you a member of **Heartsong Presents**? ❑ Yes ❑ No
   If no, where did you purchase this book? _____

   _____

3. How would you rate, on a scale from 1 (poor) to 5 (superior),
   the cover design? _____

4. On a scale from 1 (poor) to 10 (superior), please rate the
   following elements.

   ____ Heroine   ____ Plot
   ____ Hero   ____ Inspirational theme
   ____ Setting   ____ Secondary characters

6. How has this book inspired your life?_____

_____

_____

7. What settings would you like to see covered in future
   Heartsong Presents books? _____

_____

_____

8. What are some inspirational themes you would like to see
   treated in future books? _____

_____

_____

9. Would you be interested in reading other **Heartsong
   Presents** titles? ❏ Yes   ❏ No

10. Please check your age range:
    ❏ Under 18   ❏ 18-24
    ❏ 25-34   ❏ 35-45
    ❏ 46-55   ❏ Over 55

Name_____

Occupation _____

Address _____

City_____ State_____ Zip_____

E-mail_____

Ohio

*T*he first decade of the nineteenth century is full of promise and adventure for the infant state of Ohio. But for the three Carson sisters, it is filled with trepidation as they struggle with the loss of their parents in the battle for statehood.

What will be Kate, Annabelle, and Claire's legacy of faith and love for following generations?

Historical, paperback, 512 pages, 5 ³/₁₆" x 8"

❤ ❤ ❤ ❤ ❤ ❤ ❤ ❤ ❤ ❤ ❤ ❤ ❤ ❤ ❤ ❤

❤ ❤ ❤ ❤ ❤ ❤ ❤ ❤ ❤ ❤ ❤ ❤ ❤ ❤ ❤ ❤